FACE DOWN

FACE DOWN

•

Jack Lewis

AVALON BOOKS
NEW YORK

PRINTED IN THE UNITED STATES OF AMERICA
ON ACID-FREE PAPER
BY HADDON CRAFTSMEN, BLOOMSBURG, PENNSYLVANIA

This one is for Rueselle, who knows why.

Author's Note

There is a Mojave Desert and, in its expanse, an Imperial Valley. There is an All-American Canal. The Salton Sea and the area known as the Mud Pots also exist, as do the Chocolate Mountains, the Santa Rosa Mountain Range, and the border towns of Calexico and Mexicali.

The legend of the Spanish treasure ship marooned in the desert is popular lore in the desert country even today, and there have been reports of it having been seen, always during sandstorms, which seemingly covered the elusive vessel before a proper search could be organized.

However, the town of Beale is totally a product of the author's imagination as is the county in which the community is fictionally located. Equally fictitious are all the characters in the book. Any similarities to actual persons, living or dead, and places other than those mentioned above are totally coincidental.

Prologue

Operating independently, in 1959, two engineers, Robert N. Noyce of Fairchild Semiconductors and Texas Instruments' Jack Kilby, invented what is known as the microchip.

Kilby was able to encase an integrated circuit in a single wafer of silicon, while Noyce's approach was to join the circuits by creating a transistor by means of a photolithographic process that would etch and plate a series of regions on the tiny silicon sheet. This eliminated many thousands of man-hours previously spent in soldering transistors to printed circuit boards. This approach drastically reduced the weight, size, and cost of electronic compontents and led to miniaturization of numerous products. Another scientist, Jean Hoerni, later developed a planer process that allowed volume production of silicon chips.

On a single manufactured microchip, a number of connected circuit elements, including transistors and resistors, can be fabricated. Such chips are used today in all manner of automotive and household implements. However, a special type, called a nonvolatile chip, has been developed that is unaffected by static electricity, radiation, or other known means of disrupting the operation of ordinary microchips. The nonvolatile microchip has been—and is—of special, top-secret interest to our nation's military in the development of aircraft, missiles, communications equipment, and other items of modern warfare.

Chapter One

There in the sun, the heat was drilling into my skin, and sweat started to darken my khaki shirt. There wasn't enough air stirring to even rustle the big, flat leaves on the date palms across the street in the broad square that was the city park.

I watched the yellow convertible pick up speed as it moved down the street, turned the corner, and disappeared. The driver had picked me up just outside of Yuma when I had just about decided nobody loved a hitchhiker. It had taken me five days to make it that far from Corpus Christi, and I was about all in. I really felt like sleeping across the desert, but this fellow had told me when he stopped and I loaded my one suitcase into the back seat that he wanted someone to talk to. That, of course, obligated me to stay awake and talk.

He was middle-aged, maybe in his fifties, and dressed in a khaki shirt that was almost as worn as mine. He had on a big Stetson, denim pants, and a pair of scuffed engineer boots, and said he was a grape rancher from near Sacramento. He offered to take me that far, but when I told him

I was about broke and wanted to work long enough to get a stake before I went on to San Francisco, he shook his head. "There's no work around there this time of the year. They're looking for men down around Beale, though. A lot of irrigation work going on."

"They wouldn't be doing any harvesting, would they?" I asked.

"Some. But you'll more likely find a job driving a tractor or something. They're sure leveling a lot of land, getting ready to irrigate some more of that desert country. They'll have this whole darn Imperial Valley under cultivation before they're done."

"If the Colorado River doesn't run dry first. There's an awful lot of dry sand down here."

He laughed at that. He dropped me in Beale and I stood there in the street watching him disappear around the corner.

It didn't look much like a boomtown. In the park, several Mexican kids were playing, and down near the end of the street three men were unloading a truck in front of a store. A three-story brick structure featuring 1890s architecture stood at the end of the square. The rancher had mentioned that this was a county seat, so that building had to be the county courthouse.

Lots of cars, most covered with desert dust, were parked around the square, but there were few people in evidence. I could see all four sides of the park, and there were only eleven people visible. I counted them as I jingled the change I had in my pockets.

I'd gotten out of the car in front of a hotel. There were two of them in town, but the rancher had said this was the

larger and the better. The other was across the square huddled between a grocery store and a fertilizer business.

I picked up my suitcase and moved onto the sidewalk.
Even in the shade of the hotel building, it was just as hot.
Through the big plate-glass window, the man behind the
desk, a little, dried-up, bald fellow, looked like he'd spent
too much time in the sun. Head down, writing in the register, he was round-shouldered and tired.

Inside, the air-conditioning was cool. I felt as though I
had walked out of an Indian sweat lodge into an Alaskan
igloo with one swift jump. The desk clerk looked up as I
walked up to the desk and set my bag on the floor.

"Want a room, young feller?" He pushed the pen holder
toward me, then looked surprised when I shook my head.

"Not right now. I'd like to leave my suitcase here till I
look around a little. We'll talk room when I come back."

"Sure. Leave it right there. It ain't gonna run off long
as I'm here." I was almost to the door when he yelled after
me, "Want that room? Only got one left."

"Yeah. Hold it. I'll be back in a little while."

I took the money out of my pocket and looked at it.
Three singles, a half-dollar, a dime, a nickel, and four pen-
nies. The hotel bar was off the lobby. As in many small
towns, this seemed to be the social center as well as a
saloon. Several people sat in pairs and threes at tables, but
I was the only one at the bar.

Coffee was heating on the back bar. The pot was nearly
full, so I figured it had to be reasonably fresh. I ordered a
cup.

"Any idea where a man could get a job?" I asked the
bartender. "I heard there's an irrigation project of some
kind around here."

He shook his head. "I don't know much about it, but Chet Riggson's levelin' a lot of land for irrigation. Hear he's havin' trouble findin' men who'll work in 120-degree heat."

"Where is he?"

"Got an office down the street about four doors. If he isn't there, his secretary'll tell you whatever there is to know."

The single-story frame building had a large plate-glass window given an air of modesty by a venetian blind that backed the words *Chester J. Riggson, Real Estate & Land Development.* The gold lettering was old, and one of the Rs was beginning to peel off.

I pushed through the door and waited for the young woman at the desk to look up. The place was divided into two rooms. The woman, the desk, and a computer on a steel stand were on one side of the room, while the other wall was lined with filing cabinets. A calendar bearing the advertising of a manufacturer of office supplies was on the wall over the files. Through the other door, I could see a pair of black alligator cowboy boots resting on the corner of a desk.

"Can I help you?" The girl closed a ledger and stood up. Most women don't stare, especially if you stare back. She stood there half smiling, waiting for me to say something.

What I saw was nice: black eyes and hair, a tanned, oval-shaped face, and a beauty that deserved better than the cotton print dress she was wearing.

"Yes, ma'am." I looked past her at the boots on the desk. "I came to see Mr. Riggson, if he isn't too busy."

She had a little scar over one eyebrow, running down

into the hair, leaving a white streak as if the brow had been parted with a comb. I wondered how she got it.

She turned and looked at the boots. "Chet, are you busy?"

"Send him in. I heard what he said." The voice was deep and gruff, and brushing past the girl, I could see why. Riggson was a big man. Not fat, just big. Besides the boots, he had on a pair of blue jeans, one of those fancy, Mexican-made belts with all the silver mountings and studs, and a brown heavy flannel shirt. The first thing I thought of was a story a teacher had told me while I was still in grade school. It was about how the Arabs wore heavy wool clothing all the time and were able to keep the heat away from their bodies that way, shutting it out. He had a pipe in his hand, but he put it down when he saw me.

The only way of describing his face was to call it flat—broad and deep, with a nose that looked like something out of a third-rate fight club. His grayish-blond hair was cut short in military style, increasing the flat effect. He grinned and pointed to the swivel chair facing his desk.

"Sit down. What can I do for you?"

Riggson didn't offer to shake hands. He didn't even take his feet off the desk. Instead, he picked up his pipe again and started blowing on it, trying to clear the stem. I sat.

"I'm looking for work. Some folks around town said to see you." I watched as he finally pulled the pipe stem loose and looked through it. "They said you need men."

"Not just any men." He looked at me. His eyes were yellowish-brown and seemed entirely expressionless until he smiled. "I can probably use you if you know somethin' about runnin' tractors."

I nodded. "I ran one for a while in the Marines."

"Bulldozers?"

I nodded again. "Yeah."

"I'm payin' eighty bucks a day for eight hours. It sure as heck ain't union scale, but it's what I can afford." He swung his feet down from the desk and leaned forward, changing from an easygoing hulk whose only interest was a dirty pipe to a man who sounded like a Kentucky horse trader.

"We're runnin' a twenty-four-hour day. Three shifts. You'll go on at eight tonight and you'll have a man out there to relieve you at four in the morning. The third man relieves him at noon and runs again until eight o'clock that night. That's the way we work it."

"This dozer has lights for night work?"

"Sure. You'll trade with someone on another shift about every third day or so. That way, no one spends too many days workin' in that afternoon sun. That can be a real killer!"

I thought about the hot temperature and wondered what it would be like coupled with the heat blowing back from a hot motor. Silently, I wished I'd gone on up the road with the grape rancher. The heat wouldn't be as bad around Sacramento and there would be work of some kind even in the slack season.

"You got a place to stay?" The big man was looking at my sweat-stained shirt and day-old beard. "I saw you get out of that yellow car."

"I left my gear at the hotel up the block. The clerk said he had a room he'd save."

"How much money you got?"

"Not enough to pay for the room," I admitted. He knew I was going to hit him for an advance. "I was hoping you could advance me a couple of days' pay for the room and some chow.''

He looked even bigger when he stood up. He pulled a calfskin wallet out of his hip pocket and counted out five ten-dollar bills. They were all new, their green crispness broken only in the middle where the wallet folded. He doubled them up and pressed the fold into a tight crease.

''That's fifty bucks in advance.'' He held out the bills and I took them.

''Thanks. This'll pull me out of a hole.''

''Don't try to jump town. My brother-in-law's the deputy sheriff.'' He laughed when he said it, but I'd learned long ago that people don't say such things to strangers unless they mean it.

I shook my head. ''I'll be around.''

''By the way, maybe it'd be good if we got to know each other.'' He stuck out his hand. ''I'm Chet Riggson, but I guess you know that.''

''Sam Light.'' I thought I had big hands, but with him it was like shaking hands with a middle-aged octopus. I hadn't told him my name when I had come in, but I'd been so surprised at his size that I'd forgotten all about introductions.

He reached in a desk drawer to bring out a bottle of Old Granddad. ''How 'bout a drink to seal the deal?'' he offered.

I shook my head. ''Don't use the stuff. But thanks.''

Riggson cast me a quizzical glance. ''Know what they say down in Texas? Never trust a man that don't drink.''

I forced a knowing grin. ''I've known some drunken Texans I didn't trust. It all works out.''

Chuckling, he followed me into the front office where

the girl was sitting. All I'd seen earlier was her face. She didn't look up until Riggson spoke to her.

"Carol, this man's on our payroll startin' now. Name's Sam Light." He jerked his head toward me, then looked from one to the other of us. "Sam, this is Carol Kirby. He can fill out all the income tax nonsense tomorrow. He'll go on tonight, but he needs time now to get a room and get squared away." He glanced at me. "The crew boss'll pick you up at the hotel at seven o'clock."

"Got it," I told him, then turned back to Carol Kirby. She looked up at me and nodded, staring at me the same way she had before.

"Glad to know you, Mr. Light."

I returned her nod. "The feeling's mutual." She didn't smile at all, and after telling Riggson I was going to the hotel, I stepped out into the heat. I'd have preferred to sit in the coolness of the office and have Carol Kirby tell me how to fill out the goverment forms.

I saw the old man as soon as I stepped out the door and was greeted by a blast of what should have been a breeze. He was over in the square, leaning against a palm tree, watching two Mexican kids wrestle. He was a small, skinny man with a gray beard, stooped shoulders, and an old black hat. There was nothing to say about his clothes except that they covered him and pretty much matched the gray of his beard.

As I came out of Riggson's office, the old man suddenly lost interest in the fight and started across the street, following a line toward the hotel. In spite of his thinness and weak appearance, he moved swiftly, seeming to bounce along on his feet. Just the way he walked reminded me of a child sauntering home from school, swinging his books at the end of a strap.

I went into the hotel and he walked on past the big front window, looking in at me.

"Come back for that room?" the desk clerk asked, grinning at me over his glasses. I couldn't help thinking how much he and the man with the gray clothes and the beard looked alike. Not in face or features, but in general build. Skinny, round-shouldered, and dried up.

"I'll take it. Who was that fellow just looking in the window?"

"Old feller with a beard? Hickory Taite. He's just another one of the desert rats that hang around town." He giggled like an old maid. "He's given up looking for the pot of gold. Now he's happy just lookin' for the rainbow."

"Crazy?"

The clerk shook has head. "No. Not yet, anyway. He just gets peculiar ideas sometimes."

I picked up my suitcase and he slipped under the open end of the counter, a key in his hand.

"Givin' you number fourteen. Riggson told me to book you in."

"What's he got to do with it?"

"He owns the place. Chet owns half the town!" He bit at his words as if he didn't like them.

"I thought you only had one room left," I reminded him.

He flashed his false pearly whites and quickly changed the subject.

"Chet told me not to charge you for it. He'll take it out of your wages after you've started working."

We went up the stairway that passed the desk and down

a long hall to the end of the building. He stopped at the last room, fitting the key into the lock.

There was a back stairway running down to the first floor. At the foot, I could see a screen door that opened onto a wooden loading dock. Through the window at the end of the hall, I could see the alley I assumed not only ran behind the hotel but the other buildings facing the main street.

After rattling at the lock for several seconds, the clerk finally got the door open. He muttered a four-letter word as a blast of hot air hit us. "Fool idiot went off and left a window open again."

He whipped across the room and slammed down the open window while I dropped my suitcase and looked around. It wasn't a bad room. It was on a corner of the building and had windows on two sides. There was a closet, a bath, a bureau, two chairs, and a bed. That was enough. The bed was the main thing.

I went over to the window and looked out. One window looked out on the alley running behind the building, while the other looked down on one of the side streets running off the square. The hotel building was on a corner, and a wide veranda ran around the three open sides, the fourth side being built flush against the building next door.

Outside my windows was a wide, high-railed sundeck, which served as a roof for the first-story veranda. Idly I wondered why a person would want a sun deck in this country.

"Guess everything's okay, ain't it?" The old man looked around the room. "This place'll cool off soon's the air-conditioning blows all this hot air out."

"Yeah. It's okay."

It was too hot to sleep, even as tired as I was, so I followed him out and locked the door behind me. Besides, I hadn't eaten.

I found a little place on the other side of the square where the food looked pretty good. It was run by an old Mexican and two young girls I took to be his daughters.

I had roast beef, potatoes, peas, some kind of a salad, and coffee. When I finished, I was sweating again. I should have eaten a cold meal.

I walked back across the square to the hotel, noticing that the grass was turning brown. They probably had to water it every day, and some of the spots didn't get enough moisture.

In the hotel bar, it was dark and cool, and I was ordering another cup of coffee before I noticed the old man again. He was at the other end of the bar watching me, twisting a half-empty glass in little circles on the polished wood.

I eyed his reflection in the mirror behind the bar and wasn't half through with my coffee before he came over and sat down on the stool next to me. Except for the bartender who was busy polishing glasses, we were the only ones at the bar. Two women in a back booth were mumbling to each other over cold bottles of beer.

The old man had brought his drink with him and finished it before he said anything.

"You're new around here," he accused, as he wiped his hand across his mouth, then stared at my reflection in the mirror.

"Yep. Got in a little while ago."

He nodded. "I seen ya get outta that yeller car."

He'd seen me come out of Riggson's office, too, and he'd watched me go into the hotel.

"Workin' for Chet Riggson, are ya?"

"Yeah. Going to work on this land-leveling thing of his."

"How 'bout buyin' you a drink?"

I glanced into the coffee cup. It was almost empty. I shook my head. "I'm okay with this."

He ordered and paid with a handful of crumpled singles. He was drinking whiskey and water.

"Ever hear about the treasure ship out here on the Salton Sea?" He tilted his head looking at me as he asked the question.

"Not that I remember."

I'd seen the Salton Sea before, and we were only five or six miles from it then. Lots of movie companies use it and several resorts boasting only little success have been built around the edge. It's a body of salt water about forty miles long and twenty or so wide. I remembered that much from reading about how some big company made a picture about a bunch of people shipwrecked on a desert island down there once. I didn't remember anything about the picture or what it was about, but I did remember reading about the Salton Sea.

"One old Indian legends says the sea used to be part of the Gulf of Lower California till there come an earthquake." He looked at me to see if I was listening. "That range of mountains runnin' down past Mexicali's what happened. The quake cut this sea clear off from the rest of the Gulf.

"Accordin' to the story the Indians tell even now, a Spanish treasure ship was sailin' around up here, and after the earthquake, there wasn't nothin' its crew could do but just sail around and around, lookin' for a way to get out. Finally, they ran the ship on the rocks and it sank.

"Nobody ever took much stock in that story, till twenty-odd years ago, a Mexican kid came staggerin' out of the desert near dead from the heat, ravin' how he'd found a shipload of pearls out in the desert. He kept talkin' about it even after he got his head back on his shoulders. He spent the next three years lookin'. Finally went crazy an' slit his own throat."

The old man drained his glass in one quick gulp. Then he turned and looked at me, grinning.

"I'm the only one in the world that knows where that shipload of pearls is. It's there, only it ain't where most people've always looked."

I looked at his eyes for the first time. They were kind of a watery blue, the whites shot with thin red bloodlines. He looked drunk and he sounded drunk. Drunk or crazy!

Without another word, he slid off his stool and walked out the door. The bartender leaned against the bar, shaking his head.

"Old Hickory tellin' you how he's found the lost treasure ship?"

I nodded. "Yeah."

"He's told everyone in town by now. That's the third time today I've heard it."

I looked at my watch and saw it was almost 4:00. My room was probably cool enough to catch a little sleep before going to work.

I walked across the square to a drugstore where I bought a tube of shaving cream and a new toothbrush. I was starting out the door when I saw Carol Kirby coming across the square.

The cotton print dress flared at the waist, allowing the skirt to swing loosely as she walked. Her legs were long and tanned in her flat moccasins.

She crossed the street and was on the sidewalk before she saw me.

"Hi. What're you doing here?" I asked. It was a pretty lame approach.

"Through for the day. I'm going home. What're you up to?" She looked down at the package in my hand.

"Had to get some shaving cream so I can chop off my whiskers, look less like a hobo." I laughed and she laughed with me. Her teeth were white and even; her mouth turned up at the corners, bringing out a dimple in her left cheek.

"Think you're going to like your new job?"

"I guess. Sure don't know about this heat, though."

She looked at my wet shirt and smiled again. "You'll get used to it."

As she went into the store, I started across the park. As I wandered into the hotel lobby, the clerk came scuttling down the stairs like a scared crab and ducked behind the desk. He looked up and stared at me as I walked up.

The window at the end of the hall, the one looking out over the alley, was open, and a hot, stifling breeze crept to meet me. I remembered the clerk accusing someone earlier of leaving the window in my room open. It was getting to be a habit.

My door was unlocked, and I pushed it open. There were other people in the room, but the only thing I really saw was the thin, gray body lying facedown on my bed, a long silver-colored knife handle sticking out of his back. The handle was carved in the shape of a dragon's head. As I stared at it, the heat from the hall seemed to follow me in the door and wrap itself around me.

Chapter Two

"Better not move, feller," someone said behind me, but I didn't look around. The turquoise spots serving as eyes in that silver dragon's head were looking straight at me. The knife blade was buried in the man's back clear to the polished brass hilt. That and the red-soaked sheet underneath the body caused goose pimples to pop up beneath the sweat on my arms and the back of my neck. Dully, I realized I was squeezing the new tube of shaving cream I had just bought into a twisted, shapeless mass. I'd seen dead men before, but never in my own bed.

I finally looked around and saw the two men. The one pointing the pistol at me looked like a copy of a sheriff straight out of a third-rate Western movie. A big, sand-colored Stetson, denim shirt and pants, high-heeled boots, and a scuffed but well-oiled pistol belt were the first things I noticed about him. There was a big star pinned on his left shirt pocket.

The other man wore his badge under his coat lapel, and I could barely see a point sticking out. He had on a tan gabardine suit, a white shirt, and a yellow tie.

17

"What happened?" I demanded. My voice sounded like it was filtered through a bucket of gravel. I had stopped sweating suddenly, or at least I felt I had. My skin felt dry. So did my mouth. It was a stupid question to ask, but it was the only thing I could think of.

"Pretty plain, ain't it? There's a dead man in your bed." The sheriff sounded as if he'd gargled with a handful of desert sand. His voice was low and rough, as if the wind and heat had dried out his vocal cords.

"We'd kind of like to know how it got there." He said it slowly, glancing at the corpse, then back to me, without ever shifting the aim of his blued revolver. The muzzle looked like that of a .45 Colt or a .44 Magnum. The man in the suit, younger and thinner, grinned a little.

They seemed too darned calm and collected about the whole thing. I didn't like any part of it—the corpse, the way the sheriff spoke, or the way he looked at me. I didn't like that six-gun, either.

"Might as well tell you, Light, you're under arrest and anything you say'll prob'ly be used against you." I wasn't sure, but I thought I heard something more than just the coarse, rough tones. He sounded tired, as if this was something he hadn't asked for and couldn't understand why it had happened.

He wasn't a young man—in his sixties, I guessed. His hair was white below his hat, and there were deep lines cut into the tan of his forehead and cheeks. I didn't say anything, and he jerked his head toward his deputy.

"Better take him down and lock him up till we get things cleared up here, Jeff. Just for safekeeping."

The suited deputy nodded and motioned me toward the door. As his jacket swung back, I could see the cross-draw holster on his belt and the short-barreled revolver it sheathed. It was pretty obvious he didn't think I was going to run, but he was prepared if I did.

There were people all over the sidewalk outside of the hotel, and the little clerk was having trouble keeping them from pushing into the lobby.

The news had traveled fast.

They made way for me and the deputy following behind. They cleared a path across the sidewalk, then stood staring at me as I walked past.

"This the one that done it, Jeff?" someone asked.

"Too soon to tell. Don't know enough about it yet," the deputy answered. I couldn't hear what was said as we walked across the street and started across the square, but I could hear the low mutterings.

There was some relief in knowing I hadn't yet been convicted in the minds of the local law, but I remembered a movie about a mob that hanged an innocent man who was being held on a murder charge. I no longer noticed the heat.

The sheriff's office and the jail were on the corner just down from the drugstore where I'd bought the shaving cream. I had expected to be herded to the courthouse, but maybe expansion born of progress had forced the sheriff into other quarters. Whatever the reason, the sheriff's department was a long, low brick building with a couple of offices in front and a block of four cells in the back.

The deputy led me back through the offices and motioned me into one of the cells. He locked the door and went away without saying anything. I sat down on the edge of one of the two steel bunks and looked around.

There was nothing in the cell except the two bunks and a seatless toilet. Standard furnishings. The only wall was the brick of the building itself, and the other three sides of the cell were steel bars set in the concrete floor. There was one small, barred window. About then, I realized that the outer offices were air-conditioned. The cell block was not.

The deputy was stupid, I decided, as I sat there staring at the bars. He hadn't even bothered to search me. He had just brought me across the street and pushed me into a cell. I could have been packing a cannon! Then I remembered his easy confidence and that revolver angled for a fast draw from beneath his coat.

I stretched out on the bunk and looked up at the ceiling. There was nothing I could do. There was a dead man in my bed across the street, I was locked up in jail, and the fact that all I wanted was to get to San Francisco wasn't going to mean much to anyone else.

It'd all happened in less than two hours. The grape rancher had let me out, I'd had some coffee, gotten a job, met a girl, heard a story about a treasure ship out in the middle of the desert, and walked in on the murder of the man who told it!

It was hot in the cell, and as I lay there staring up at the ceiling, the sweat ran off my nose and into my eyes. I wiped it off with my fist. A murmur of voices seemed to be coming from one of the offices. I couldn't hear what was being said, but I could tell two men were talking. The tones of one echoed anger and the other guy was trying to calm him down, talking slowly and soothingly. Another door slammed and I couldn't hear the voices anymore. Apparently the two had gone out. I tried to analyze the voices, remember whether I'd heard either one of them before. If I had, the door had muffled any recognizable traits. I had to assume it was the old sheriff and the deputy.

I dropped back on the bunk again, and looked up at the ceiling. There was a spider web in the corner near the little barred window, and I could see three dead flies and a spider huddled together there in a black group.

I thought about the job Johnny Ferguson was supposed to be holding for me, and I wondered about the little gray man lying dead in my bed. After six months of it, I had come to realize hoboing was not the adventurous or romantic thing some earlier writers had pictured. I was ready to start working. Now this mess had to happen!

I sat up and lit a cigarette, wiping more sweat off my face with a shirt sleeve. I suddenly realized I resented the man who had called himself Hickory Taite. I resented the way he had died. I resented the grape rancher in the yellow car, too. If I'd stayed in the car, I would still be on my way north. Johnny'd have staked me if I'd really needed money when I hit his town, but I'd had this fool idea about earning enough to tide myself over. Over the years, pride had gotten me into a lot of trouble.

It'd been the same way when I'd got out of the Marines after the Gulf War. Johnny had wanted me to come to work immediately on the *Citizen*, but I'd had to go off hoboing, seeing the world on a shoestring, with notions about becoming another Jim Tully, writing novels about life on the open road.

Up on the ceiling, the spider moved across the web to the wall and settled there. A breeze came through the window and rocked the web back and forth, causing the strands to sparkle a reddish-blur then silver in the light.

I must have gone to sleep for a minute. I stood up when I heard the sheriff unlocking the cell door.

"Come on, Light," he said. "We're gonna ask you some questions."

I tossed my burned-out cigarette butt in the seatless toilet before I walked out. He followed me through the first door and motioned me into one of the offices. The deputy named Jeff and Chet Riggson were there. Jeff was sitting behind a desk covered with papers. There was an ink stand and a calendar topped by two-inch plaster images of three monkeys: SEE NO EVIL, HEAR NO EVIL, and SPEAK NO EVIL. Riggson was staring out the window facing the square.

"Sit down, Sam," the sheriff ordered. He pointed to a chair at one corner of the desk. I sat down and waited. I tried not to look worried, but I knew I wasn't succeeding.

"You got into town this afternoon, didn't you, Light?" the deputy asked. He wasn't looking at me. He was looking down at his desk, seeming to concentrate on the clutter of papers.

"Aren't you going to read me my rights?" I asked.

"We're just going to ask you some questions and turn you loose." Jeff still didn't look up from the papers. Riggson turned away from the window and looked at me for a second before he spoke. His face was red and there was just a hint of moisture on his forehead.

"I've identified the knife, Sam." He turned and scouled at Jeff. "It's one of a set of three that was stolen from me a couple of weeks ago."

I looked at him, then at Jeff and, finally, the sheriff. I felt like laughing, but I didn't. I was afraid it would sound like hysteria.

Chapter Three

Riggson nodded, that half-smile still on his lips. "The knife belongs to me. That fool kid stole all three of 'em."

"One of the Mexicans he had workin' around the hotel," the sheriff explained, jerking his head toward the window and the square beyond.

Nothing they'd said was too clear, but it sounded as if Riggson had owned a set of three dragon-head knives, they'd been stolen by some Mexican kid, and one of them had ended up in old Hickory's back. I wondered what had become of the other two daggers.

"We want to find out just where you fit into this mess. You're pretty much in the clear from what Chet's told us, but you're still involved." Jeff looked up amiably. "It was your room."

"What's all this make me? A witness?"

Jeff nodded. "Something like that. You may not think it's strictly legal, but we want you to hang around town until this thing starts to make sense. Chet says you're to start working for him, so go ahead and work, but we want you where we can find you."

I looked at the sheriff, then at Jeff. The older man—I still didn't know his name—was leaning against the door, rolling a cigarette and looking as though he had no interest in what was being said.

"Where'd you come from?" the deputy asked. He leaned across the desk, looking at me, and the lapel of his coat slid up enough to reveal the entire badge pinned above his shirt pocket.

"Left Yuma this morning. Caught a ride this far with a grape-grower."

"Where'd you come from before that? Where was the last place you worked?"

"Miami. I left there eight days ago."

"Hitchhiking?"

I nodded.

"What'd you do in Miami?" Jeff leaned back in his swivel chair and looked in his coat pockets for a cigarette. He finally found a crushed pack in an inside pocket.

"Picked oranges for a while. Tended bar for two weeks."

Riggson turned his back on the room to gaze out the window again. The deputy smoothed out his wrinkled cigarette by pulling at the ends and lit it.

"Where'd you tend this bar?" That was the first question the sheriff had asked.

"It's just a little place called the Buckhorn. Guy named Tony Scarpello owns it."

Jeff took a drag off his cigarette and pushed the pack across the desk toward me. He wrote down Scarpello's name and the name of the bar on one of the blank scraps of paper while I lit up.

"Where're you headed now, Light?"

"San Francisco."

"What's there? Anything?"

I nodded. It was kind of hard to figure. Before Jeff had shoved me into that cell, he hadn't even bothered to search me, and I'd decided he was either stupid or dangerously overconfident. Now he was doing all the questioning, while the boss just stood there with his back against the door, hardly opening his mouth. Actually, nobody seemed to be taking this thing very seriously.

"What's waiting for you in San Francisco?" Jeff asked again, his tone a little less casual.

"A newspaper job, I hope."

The sheriff straightened from his position against the door frame and stared at me. When I looked back to the deputy, I knew neither of them believed me.

"What paper?" he asked.

"The San Francisco *Citizen*. An old friend of mine's the managing editor. John T. Ferguson. I worked with him back East."

Jeff wrote some more on his slip of paper after asking how to spell Johnny's last name. I told him.

"You need me for anything more?" Riggson asked. He didn't turn away from the window when he spoke, but kept looking out across the street and the square. Either he was watching for someone or was bored with the whole affair.

"You're sure there's no way Light here could've gotten hold of the knife." The sheriff spoke in statements, not questions.

Riggson nodded, turning away from the window. It was getting dark fast. The clock on the wall behind Jeff's desk said ten minutes till seven.

"Sam, when they're done with you, come over to the

hotel. I want to talk to you." Riggson looked at the sheriff. "You'll want me to have that room closed up, won't you? I can have the clerk find another room for Light here."

"One of us'll be over to put a seal on the door," Jeff told him.

The clerk had told me only hours earlier that I was renting the last room in the hotel. Riggson wasn't going to lose any money as long as he had that dried-up runt peddling rooms! "Yeah," the sheriff put in. "We ain't gonna want nobody foolin' around in there till we've had plenty of time to look it over. Give him another room and lock that one till we get back over there."

The deputy folded the piece of paper carrying his notes and stuck it in his shirt pocket. Riggson closed the door behind himself, allowing the sheriff to settle against the doorjamb, again.

"You tell a pretty straight story, Light." Jeff tapped his pocket holding his notes. "But we're going to check with this Scarpello. We'll check on this job of yours in San Francisco, too, just to keep the record straight."

I shrugged. "I'll be around."

The sheriff nodded. "We'll know where to find you."

I had no intention of leaving town. I had to get in touch with Johnny Ferguson. This was a story no other reporter in the country would know about yet, and I was right on the spot. I could see my job starting before I ever got to the Golden Gate. I was going to start right here, reporting on this murder. Working nights for Riggson, I'd have my days to do a different kind of digging. Riggson had influence in town, and I'd be able to pick up a lot from him. If other papers sent reporters to cover the story, I'd still have the best sources of information. I glanced at the clock again, and Jeff shook his head. It was 7:00 on the nose.

"Chet's not going to send you out there to work tonight. He knows this mess is pretty much of a strain. Probably a strain on him, too, having a guy he's been grubstaking for years get knocked off. He'll probably halt operations altogether for a day or so, until things settle down a little."

Outside, the streetlights went on and I squirmed in the straight-backed chair. They weren't asking me any real questions, but they still weren't ready to let me go. They were fishing in the dark, not knowing what to say or ask, just making small talk to fill in the gaps.

"If that's all you need from me, I'm going to see what Riggson wants," I announced, rising.

Jeff leaned back in his chair and yawned.

"I guess we're done for now," he said, holding his fist over his mouth.

I walked across the square in the dim light and learned from the desk clerk that my stuff had been moved into another room. I gave him the key to my old room and he exchanged it, then I headed for the bar.

Riggson was talking to one of the bartenders. The place was full, and two white-shirted men were juggling drinks. A young woman flitted from table to table with a tray. Her back was to me, so I couldn't see her face.

I elbowed a place at the bar beside Riggson and waited for him to finish his drink. He didn't notice me until I spoke.

"You wanted to see me, Mr. Riggson?" I asked. There were too many people in the place, and even with the air-conditioning it was hot. It was a different kind of heat. Outside, it was hot and dry. This was damp and smelly.

Most of the people standing at the bar wore work clothes, and the odor of dried sweat was even heavier than the smell of liquor.

Riggson stared at my reflection in the big mirror on the wall behind the bar. "My brother-in-law and that old goat finally get done with you?"

I'd almost forgotten he'd told me earlier that the deputy was his brother-in-law. He'd mentioned it when he'd given me the advance on my wages.

"There wasn't much I could tell them."

Riggson nodded. "I had to argue with those fools for near onto an hour before I finally convinced 'em you couldn't have had anything to do with it. What'd they ask you?"

"I gave them a brief outline of my life history, and they told me I'd better stick around until they find out who's sticking knives in people."

"Neither one of 'em can find a stolen burro, let alone catch a murderer. Gould knows he's stupid, and he lets Jeff handle things. Trouble is, Jeff's just as stupid and don't know it."

"Gould the sheriff?"

"Yeah. Barney Gould's been sheriff for the last eighteen years."

The bartender scooped up Riggson's empty glass and stood looking at us expectantly.

"I'll take Coke," I told him.

I wanted to get away to a telephone. The sooner I reached Johnny Ferguson, the better.

"You prob'ly don't feel much like work tonight, do you?"

I shook my head. "I'd just as soon not, if it's okay. I feel clear beat out."

"I already sent a kid out to the job to tell Jim Teckwell to close down. We won't work tonight at all."

"Tell me a little bit about this land-leveling stuff," I suggested.

He shifted his weight on the stool. "What we're doing is levelin' a lot of desert up north of here so we can run irrigation ditches through it and turn it into farmland. It's good soil and all it needs to make it productive is water."

"You own the land, or working it over for someone else?"

"I own it. I inherited the stuff several years ago after my wife died. I didn't think it'd ever be good for nothin', but this irrigation water bein' brought from the Colorado River has turned the whole thing into a gold mine."

"You're farming the stuff yourself?"

"Part of it. I'll farm it the first year, growing either rice or alfalfa, and the second year, I'll sell. Once I've proved the ground'll raise crops. I'll be sellin' to small-grain farmers."

I was tempted to drop the other conversational shoe by asking how much of the Colorado River water he felt he could get. I had read somewhere that the water supply had such high usage that the states of California and Arizona were starting to battle over water rights. But I decided to leave well enough alone.

"You said you know about tractors." Riggson looked at me sharply, as if he thought I might have been lying earlier about my hands-on experience.

I nodded. "Pushed some dirt around digging out mine-fields while in the service."

Riggson nodded his approval. "If you can handle stuff like that, you for certain know enough to handle this job."

He finished his drink and set the glass on the bar. He said something, but I didn't hear what it was. I'd suddenly caught a reflection in the mirror—the waitress I'd noticed when I'd come in was staring.

She was a tall blond with a long, thin face. Even in the dim light, I could see the heavy mascara and the gray-green shadow under her eyes. She wore suntan makeup and a shade of lipstick that was just a little too red.

I couldn't tell whether she was staring at Riggson or me, but there was no doubt about her expression. I'd only seen it once before—on the faces of two women in a bar in Juarez who'd been fighting over a man. It was pure hatred.

The kind of look only a woman can have.

Chapter Four

"Y̲ou need a refill?"

I glanced at the bartender just long enough to shake my head, but when I looked back at the mirror again, the blond had turned her back and was waiting on one of the tables.

I thought of asking Riggson about her, but there were too many other things I wanted to know before I put in my phone call to San Francisco. The bartender brought Riggson's drink and I pushed my glass in front of him.

"On second throught, maybe you'd better fill that up again."

"Plain Coke." It was a positive announcement, verifying something he already knew.

"Right."

"The whole town's talkin'." Riggson glanced around the room. "I'd hate to be in that kid's shoes if they ever catch him."

"The one who stole your knives?"

"Petey Basquez. He did odd jobs around here. When them knives disappeared out of the office, he was the only one who could've took 'em."

"You're not totally sure he took them then?" I hoped I didn't sound like a district attorney questioning a witness.

"There wasn't really any proof. Just opportunity. He denied he took them, and I just fired him. They weren't worth enough to cause a lot of trouble."

"Where do you think this kid might be? Why would he want to kill the old man?"

My thoughts cycled back to the treasure story Taite had told me and about the Mexican who claimed to have found the Spanish ship, then killed himself. Could there be a connection between him and Basquez?

"Petey?" Riggson shook his head. "Jeff and Gould haven't been able to find him. He stayed with his sister, but she says she hasn't seen him since the day I canned him."

I paid for both drinks before I asked him about the murdered man. "What was this old man's real name, Chet?"

"Taite? If he had a first name, I never heard it. Everyone just called him Hickory."

I was watching the waitress. Jeff had come in and was standing just inside the door. The girl was talking to him and glancing in my direction from time to time. I still couldn't tell whether she was watching Riggson or me. I didn't hear what the big man said and had to ask him to repeat it.

"This deal's gonna hurt the hotel business for a while. At least till people forget about it a little and maybe realize they won't be murdered in their beds."

"Aren't most of your guests like me? Drifters?"

"Nope. Most everybody livin' here has a business right here in town, or works steady for someone. That other place across the square gets most of the fruit tramps passin' through.''

''Most of these people knew Hickory Taite?''

Riggson took his old black pipe out of his trousers pocket and tapped it on the heel of one of his boots before he answered my question.

''Yeah. He spends most of his time around here when he's not out in the desert. Guess most everyone knows him by sight.''

I started to point out that he better start referring to Taite in the past tense, but I changed my mind.

''Yeah.'' He started to fill his pipe, but stopped and looked at me. ''Just about everyone in my hotel's a suspect. Can't hardly blame 'em if they want to move out.''

I slid off the stool and emptied my glass just before Jeff clamped his hand on my shoulder.

''Just stopped by to tell you we'll need you at the coroner's inquest tomorrow. You, too, Chet.''

''What time's it coming off?'' Riggson asked, lighting his pipe and blowing a cloud of smoke at his reflection in the mirror.

''Sometime around ten o'clock. It'll be down at the funeral parlor, same as always.''

I told the deputy I'd be there and said good night. Walking through the door that led back into the hotel lobby, I picked up my key at the desk and learned there was a telephone in my room.

''Are there telephones in all the rooms?'' I asked. The room clerk stared over his glasses at me, then looked away with a shake of his head.

''Not all of 'em.''

I went up to my newly assigned room and looked around.

It was just down the hall from the murder room and looked out over the same railed balcony and the alley behind the hotel. The room was furnished almost exactly the same, except for a telephone on a table beside the bed.

It took me about ten minutes to get through to Johnny Ferguson at home and have him agree to accept the charges. I didn't want this call to show up on my hotel bill.

"Where in blazes have you been? First I hear from you in Miami, then you're almost in Mexico!" It took me another five minutes to get him calmed down enough to bring him up to speed on what had happened.

"I think there's a real story here," I told him.

"I don't know." He was dubious. "It's a killing that's five hundred miles from our readers. We have enough violent death right here in town to satisfy their blood lust."

"But the killing isn't the angle," I insisted. "There's all that stuff about the ship in the desert, and the kid who said he found it, then slit his throat. And don't forget that Hickory Taite told me he'd found the treasure. It's a natural for a series. You might even be able to syndicate it and make some money from other papers or the tabloids."

"Well, maybe." He was still trying to sound doubtful, but I'd seen this act before. "I can't put you on the payroll until you get here and go through all the administrative garbage, but right now, I can pay you space rates for whatever we print."

By the time we hung up, Ferguson was happy as a kid with bare feet and a fishing pole. I sat there on the bed for a minute, rubbing my beard. It was beginning to itch and I wondered what I'd done with the tube of shaving cream I'd bought in the afternoon. I remembered squeezing it to pieces, but I hadn't had it when we'd gotten to the jail. I looked at myself in the mirror and decided I should shave before going to bed. I was coming out of the drugstore with my package, when I saw Carol again. I didn't think she was going to speak to me, but I tried a smile and she recriprocated.

I like her smile, and the more I saw of it, the more I liked it. I'm funny that way. Sometimes I like the way a person smiles right from the start, but too much bothers me. The smile that comes too easily doesn't mean anything. That makes me nervous.

"Haven't you shed that beard yet?" she asked.

"I've been busy."

"Everyone in town's busy, solving the crime or deciding who to hang," she said, shaking her head with what I interpreted as a grimace of distaste for what was happening.

"I hope I'm not the chief candidate." I offered a chuckle I didn't feel.

She shook her head. "You're just one of them."

Now that was a pleasant thought!

"Where're you headed?" I asked. She still had on the cotton dress she'd been wearing in the afternoon, but she'd fixed her hair differently. She'd swept it back and tied it with a blue ribbon at the back of her neck. A red ribbon, I decided, would have been better.

"I'm on my way home."

"Where do you live from here?"

She pointed down the street past the end of the square.

"I rent a room from some friends down a couple of blocks. Want to walk me?" She smiled at me again.

We walked to the end of the block without saying anything. Leaving the square, it was dark with streetlights only at the intersection.

She finally broke the silence.

"What're you doing here, Sam? You're not like the professional pea-pickers we have come through."

I stopped to look at her in the yellow rays from the streetlight on the corner.

"In reality," I told her with a laugh, "I'm your Prince Charming." I knew it was a lousy line, but I've never been good at that sort of thing.

"I'm serious. I know what the sheriff is saying, but I want to hear your version."

"The sheriff doesn't waste much time. Maybe you'd better tell me what he says first."

She shrugged a little. "This is a small town, and there's not much else for entertainment but gossip. Someone asked about you and he said you're a washed-up newspaper man turned hobo."

I nodded in agreement. "I didn't go into it far enough for him to understand."

We were standing face-to-face in front of someone's house. It was a house with a healthy green lawn and lights in the windows. That was where we sat down, there on the people's lawn.

"I was a newspaper reporter and a darn good one. I had served a hitch in the Marines, then went to college on the GI Bill. I got into the newspaper business, but what I really thought I wanted to do was write a book. Then the Gulf War came along, and I was called up as a Reservist. I was assigned to a unit as a Marine Corps Combat Correspondent and shipped off to Iraq.

"All that time, I kept kind of a notebook on things I saw that I thought I might work into my book, if I ever got a chance to write it. Then the war was over as fast as it started, and I found out no one is interested in reading about a war that lasted only a few weeks.''

She sat there with the light from the street lamp throwing long shadows over her face and just listened, watching me while I talked.

''I didn't get an idea for another book until I was ready for release from active duty. I don't even know how I got it. I just decided to turn hobo until I had enough stuff to write a novel or maybe a book of short stories about today's Knights of the Road. I even decided on a title: *The Hoboes' Handbook*.'' I looked at her again to be sure she wasn't laughing. Instead, I faced a troubled scowl. Her voice was quiet.

''You're an alcoholic, aren't you, Sam?''

I was surprised. ''Recovering alcoholic,'' I corrected. ''Three years sober. How'd you know?''

''My father was an alcoholic. I heard the defensiveness in your tone, when you talked to Riggson about Texans and drinking.''

''What about you? What're you all about?'' I wanted to know.

She sighed before she answered, looking off into the darkness. ''Not much to tell. I was born here. My dad worked in a borax plant upcounty, but he and my mom died in a car crash four days after I graduated from high school. He was drunk.'' Surprisingly, I heard no bitterness. Just facts.

''Everybody knew my folks around here and they tried to help. They took up a collection, then Chet Riggson loaned me the money to go to secretarial school in San Diego. The deal was that I would come back and work for him until I paid back the loan.''

"Isn't it paid off yet?"

She nodded. "Years ago, but it's a job. There aren't many around here. California may be the Golden State, but this is a poor county. Until they started irrigating, we had borax and not much else. Then the borax ran out. People don't really live here. They just sort of hang on, hoping things will get better."

I nodded my understanding. "I noticed Gould seems to have just himself and Street to cover a whole county. And with that office and jail he has, it looks like he was edged out of the county courthouse."

"He has a couple of more deputies," she explained, "but they operate at opposite ends of the county, so they live there and patrol there. They come into town when they must. The courthouse is more than a hundred years old, and everyone talks about building a new one, but there isn't enough money."

"You ought to get out of here," I advised.

"I know the people here." Her tone was suddenly defensive.

"And now you know me," I told her.

She hesitated for a moment, considering, then looked at me, her tone low and throaty. "I'm glad."

I took that as a cue and kissed her. She didn't pull away, and I could feel her hand rub over the whiskers on my cheek. Her breath on my face was a contrast to the coolness of her lips.

We sat there on the lawn without saying anything much until a clock struck somewhere, and she stood up. I got up and took her arm.

"Home?" I asked.

She shook her head, and glanced at the house. "This is home. We're here."

I went back to the hotel and went to bed. I didn't dream about the murder or about Carol Kirby. I didn't dream about anything. I just slept.

Chapter Five

It was almost 9:00 when I woke from what might be called the sleep of the dead, but it didn't seem appropriate at the time. I sat up on the edge of the bed and, even with the air-conditioning, I knew it was going to be another skin-scorcher. The sun was beating down and thin waves of heat were hanging close to the roof of the building across the alley.

I shaved off what beard I had grown during the night before soaking in the old-fashioned, claw-legged bathtub. My skin was still damp when I pulled fresh khakis out of my suitcase, uncovering my pistol. Packed amid several pairs of socks as protection against damage, it was a .45 1911A1 Colt I had inherited from my father. He had carried it in the Korean War, and I had packed it in the Gulf War, favoring it over one of the Beretta-made 9mm models that were being issued. It had a lot more stopping power than the 9mm.

I pondered the idea of carrying the handgun for a moment. Common sense took over, however. I was mixed up in a murder, but there was no reason I should go armed.

Besides, I didn't have a California permit for concealed-carry, and the big old hunk of iron was too heavy to be practical. I wrapped it in my dirty shirt before I shut the suitcase.

I finished dressing and was on my way down to breakfast when a young Mexican woman stopped me on the stairs. From the crumpled uniform, I assumed she was one of the hotel housekeepers. Probably the only one.

''Señor Riggson asks you to stop at his office before you go to the coroner's inquest. I was coming up to tell you.'' She smiled and pointed up the stairway behind me to emphasize the content of her statement. I thanked her and continued down the creaking stairs. The clerk wasn't at the desk, so I stuck the room key in my pocket.

Outside, I started to look at the thermometer mounted on the corner of the hotel building, then changed my mind. Knowing how hot it was officially would only make me feel worse. I cut across the square to the little place where I had eaten the previous day. I was going to have breakfast before seeing Riggson.

I was settled at one of the oilcloth-covered tables, the only customer, before I realized there was something strange going on. After several minutes, no one had come to wait on me, although three Mexican girls were huddled back in the kitchen talking in low-toned Spanish. They kept glancing in my direction, and I was at the point of finding another place, when one of them finally came out. In spite of the attitude of collective fear I seemed to generate among the trio, I finally got a couple of cheese enchiladas and some beans.

Riggson was in his office, but Carol hadn't come in yet. I felt a surge of disappointment that caused me to realize I had been looking forward to seeing her. Riggson was standing in the open back door, staring through the screen at something across the alley. There was nothing there except a long, sheet-metal building that appeared to be a warehouse. The big man didn't seem to be looking at anything specific, just standing there with his pipe in his mouth, leaning against the doorjamb.

"What're you doing besides soaking up the heat?" I asked. He turned quickly as if I'd startled him and grinned, taking his pipe out of his mouth.

"Mornin, Light. Didn't expect you so soon. Had breakfast?" He pointed to a chair.

"Just finished. Someone said you wanted to see me." I sat down and waited for him to go on.

"You all ready for this inquest?"

I nodded. "Yeah. I suppose all I'll have to tell will be how I found the body. That won't be hard with your brother-in-law and the sheriff both being there when I came in."

"I heard something this morning I thought maybe you ought to know about." He moved away form the door, still leaving it open. He looked at the bowl of his pipe and then dug at it with his finger. It was out.

"What's this?" I was puzzled by his announcement. What should I know?

"Since eight o'clock, I've heard rumors you're a private investigator lookin' for this lost treasure ship, I've heard you're a narcotics or maybe a Customs agent, and I've heard you're a crackpot newspaper man who don't give a hoot about bein' a newspaper man." He went on playing with his pipe. "The private eye part was interestin'. Theory is that you're working for the Spanish government to recover their property that's been lost for a coupla centuries.''

''You have to be kidding!'' Recalling Carol's comment about gossip being the chief source of entertainment, I was amazed. ''Where'd you hear all of this stuff?''

Riggson shook his head, still grinning. ''Can't tell you. If you were a reporter, you'd know about protecting your sources.''

''But you want to know just which one of them I am.''

''I generally like to know what goes on in this town. It helps me make a livin', if I know what's likely to happen.''

I knew he was trying to pump me, and I didn't like that. Still, I couldn't help admiring the way he'd handled it. He hadn't beat around the bush, trying to do everything but make a direct point. He'd come right out and asked me. I shrugged.

''I suppose you could call me something of a tramp journalist. Sort of what Mark Twain was in the last century, but I haven't had much luck at it. Right now I'm supposed to be working for you.''

Riggson nodded. ''You are, but you won't get anything done for me today what with this inquest and stuff.''

''No work today?''

''I don't imagine we'll get much work done till after Hickory's funeral. That's tomorrow morning. Everyone in town will be there.''

Maybe I didn't understand desert people; at least, that's what I was thinking then. It seemed odd that almost everyone in town would knock off work just because an old desert rat had been killed. ''How long did you know Taite?'' I asked.

"Ten years, maybe. Ever since I've been in this part of the country."

I looked at my wristwatch, which was about the only valuable thing I owned that wasn't in a hock shop somewhere. It was ten minutes of ten.

"About time to get over there?"

I nodded. "I guess so. This thing starts at ten, doesn't it?"

The undertaker ran a furniture store as his main line, and the mortuary/county morgue, if it could be called that, was in the store basement where the inquest was held.

There wasn't much to the place. It was nothing but a room with a few chairs and three marble slabs over against one wall. There was something on one of the slabs with a long white sheet over it. It didn't take much imagination to guess what was under the sheet.

The inquest was brief. The sheriff and his deputy told how they'd been called over to the hotel by the clerk and had been shown the body. The maid who had found it was the same one who had spoken to me earlier. She told of going to make certain there was clean linen in the room.

They hardly questioned me at all. Just asked when I'd come into town and what I'd done in the time between my arrival and the moment I'd walked into my room and found the sheriff waiting. They didn't ask about my talking to Hickory in the bar and hearing that crazy story of the shipload of pearls in the desert. And I didn't volunteer the information.

The verdict was "slain by a person or persons unknown."

Riggson and I hung around after the inquest. He wanted to talk to the undertaker, a man named Marks, about buying some furniture for his office. I waited while they discussed the price of desks and swivel chairs.

There in the clammy confines of the basement, I was standing beside that long, sheeted ridge. I couldn't resist the temptation to pull back the sheet and look. I don't get any particular joy out of looking at a corpse—any corpse— but I seemed to have a personal interest in this one. After all, he was indirectly responsible for people thinking I was a private detective, a narcotics agent, or a crackpot!

His stubbly beard had been shaved and what had seemed gray and weather-beaten was now a face full of deep, tired lines. He no longer wore the old, gray clothing. He was bare, and I wondered what clothes they were going to bury him in.

His hands were folded across his chest in orthodox fashion, and his fingers were grimy, long streaks of black under his nails. His hands needed washing.

I covered him up again and waited for Riggson and Marks to finish talking. When they were done, Riggson hadn't bought any furniture, and the other man, small and bald with a sleepy look, had given up on the sell job before we started up the stairway.

"What time's this funeral tomorrow?" I asked.

"It starts at ten, same as this morning."

I pondered those dirty-looking hands. It hadn't been dirt at all. It was ink. Black fingerprint ink. There had to be a reason why the sheriff would take the fingerprints of a dead man.

Chapter Six

Carol was in the office when we got back and seemed to be dealing with the same ledger she'd had the day before. It made me realize how much had happened in the past few hours.

She smiled as we came in. "Good morning, you two."

We both said hello, and the big man loomed over her, looking down at the leather-bound book.

"Getting my bookkeeping pretty well I squared away?"

She nodded and laughed. "I don't know how you ever managed to know how much money you have with this system of yours."

She looked at me. "What do you think about a man who devises his own method of keeping accounts, then when he wants it done right, he has to spend almost a week explaining his code?" She wrinkled her nose and dug at a blotter with the pen she was holding. I laughed, as Riggson straightened up.

"Come on back to the office, Sam. The morning calls for some small talk and for me, at least, a drink. I can have Carol rustle you up a soft drink of some kind."

46

"I don't need anything," I told him.

He had a bottle of good Scotch and a pair of water tumblers he dragged out of a desk drawer. He filled his glass almost half full of bourbon and held it up. "Sure you won't join me?" I shook my head, ignoring the nearly full bottle.

"Cheers." He tossed it off, then lowered the glass. "You one of them AA fellers? Alcoholics Anonymous?"

"I've been to some meetings," I admitted, wondering whether Carol had told him.

He nodded approval. "They do good work, I hear."

"It works for those who really want to quit."

On the walk back from the basement mortuary I'd been thinking about those fingers still dark with fingerprint ink. It wasn't hard to figure what the sheriff or his deputy had done, but they had to have a reason.

It wouldn't necessarily be for identification, because everyone around town seemed to have known the old prospector, and when he wasn't out digging at the rocks and sand, Beale seemed to be the only home he'd had. They were going to bury him here. There had to be another reason for the fingerprinting.

"Ever been in this country before?" Riggson asked. He had set his glass down and was filling his pipe.

"The only times I've come across the desert I've crossed the state line to or from Arizona at Blythe."

"Up north. Where'd you come from this time, Yuma?" I nodded in reply to the question. I was being interrogated again.

Riggson stood up and pulled down a large-scale roll map that didn't look at all familiar. I had to stand up and move closer to figure it out.

Down in the lower center was a dark area that represented the town, and on to the east, the Chocolate Mountains were designated by a series of brownish, rippling rings. The Salton Sea, a long, bulky blotch of blue, was almost in the center of the map. The rest of it was desert, except for a few more scattered settlements near the north end of the big body of water.

Riggson pointed to a spot north of the area representing Beale. Part of the area had been shaded in with a red pencil.

"That's where we're working now." Riggson ran his finger around the red. "Most of that land is already being irrigated. When it's finished, we'll move on north. I own the equipment, and we're getting most of the leveling work whether we own the ground or not." He moved his finger to a long line running the full length of the map and parallel to the Chocolate Mountain range.

"This canal irrigates all this land. The water comes out of the Colorado River and runs darn near to the border.'

He looked at me questioningly as I stood there frowning.

"What's the matter?"

"Maybe you'd better explain something to me about this land leveling thing," I said. "I don't know anything about leveling land for growing things and even less about irrigation."

Riggson sat down again and I did the same. He still hadn't lit his pipe, and he took time to do it before saying anything.

He shook out the match and dropped it on the floor.

"There's not much to it," he said. "Most of the land down here is pretty flat. You've seen that for yourself. It still needs flattening a tad more before we can run irrigation ditches through it. It all works on the old principle that water doesn't run uphill.

Riggson poured another stiff drink. It was cool there in the office, the air-conditioning unit whirling softly. I could see the sun beating down on the metal roof of the warehouse across the alley. I knew I'd soon be out there in the heat.

Riggson held his glass up and drank as he had the first time. I was glad I didn't have to keep up with him. Drinking is something I learned about the hard way.

"You were asking this morning whether I was a narcotics man, a customs agent, or a private detective after that treasure ship. What's that all about?"

"There've been half a dozen private investigators down here, digging up all the information available. There are people in L.A. and Frisco with money who believe that story. They send these guys down to listen to all the stories, then come themselves on treasure-hunting parties with a bunch of their friends." He paused and puffed at his pipe. "One summer every town around here was full of Hollywood Boulevard treasure hunters!"

I laughed. "And you thought I was going to bring another bunch of tourists storming down on you heads, huh?"

"Tourist trade's good for any town. They want the best of everything in town, and they usually get it." He laughed. "One big bunch came flocking down here, and my clerk almost sold my own room out from under me!"

I nodded. "What about the other things? Narc? Customs agent?"

"They're the first thing any stranger's likely to be figured for." He shrugged. "There're drugs and aliens coming across the border all the time. That's the case from San Diego clear to East Texas. The Border Patrol tried hard, but they can't be everywhere at the same time. Naturally, agents show up from time to time.

"Same's true of the customs people. For a while, there was big-time smuggling of cheap microchips made somewhere in the Orient. Border Patrol's got sensors buried along a lot of the border, but these people would come up to the fence in a four-wheel drive to throw suitcases full of microchips across. They'd get picked up and moved into L.A. at cut-rate prices. Played havoc with the makers up in Silcon Valley.

Silicon Valley, I knew, was the area south of San Francisco, where hundreds of electronics firms, including microchip manufacturers, were headquartered. "I'll bet any of these agencies would love to hear a hobo's been mistaken for one of their men."

"It's happened. One of them spent all summer down here, working around town just for his keep. He was found dead before any of us knew what he really was."

"That gives me a real warm, fuzzy feeling," I told him. "When I'm found with a knife in my back, you be sure to tell the whole town someone made a mistake!"

Riggson told me more about land-leveling and how eventually the water from the canal could lead to the cultivation of the whole desert east of the Salton Sea.

"It's gonna take time, but it'll happen," he concluded.

"How far from the Salton Sea are we?" I asked. I was having trouble keeping my eyes off the bottle on his desk. I wished I was somewhere else.

"It's out north, maybe six miles. You can see the water from the edge of town."

Those fingerprints still bothered me, too. All the time I had been talking to Riggson, the thought had been straining at the back of my mind, but I couldn't see just where they fit in.

"Does anyone know where the old man came from?" I asked.

Riggson looked at me, a trace of annoyance in his expression. "Who?"

"Hickory Taite."

Riggson shook his head. "Somebody may know. I don't."

"No family ties around here?" I knew I was asking too many questions, and I pushed myself up from the chair. "Let's talk later. I'd better get out of here and get some lunch."

Riggson grinned, nodding. "A little early or I'd go with you."

"See you later," I promised. As I pushed through the door to the outer office, Carol looked up. I couldn't help but smile, even if she had told her about my problem.

"How soon are you going to lunch?" I asked. She leaned back from the typewriter and ran her fingers through her hair.

"As soon as I finish this letter, get Chet to sign them, and get them ready to mail. Why?"

"I'm taking you to lunch."

"You seem pretty sure of that. Tell you what, I'll finish this stuff and meet you in the hotel. I have to drop some papers with Eddie. Okay?" I nodded agreement.

"I'll be along," she said. "Half an hour at most." The soft click of computer followed me out into the sun.

I had a Coke and tried to get a discussion going with the bartender. He was the one who had been working the bar when I'd arrived in town. He stayed at the far end of his station, though, peeling lemons and cutting the peel into strips. He would give each strip an artistic little twist, then drop it into a glass dish. I asked a couple of questions, but all I really got out of him was that his name was Eddie. I was standing in front of the jukebox, looking over the selections when Carol came in. I dropped in a quarter, punched a button without checking the selection, and turned to meet her.

"You're early," I charged.

"Mr. Riggson said he'd sign the letters and mail them when he goes to lunch. And he's bringing the stuff to Eddie, too."

She looked down at the jukebox as Garth Brooks's voice blared from the speakers, then looked up at me.

"You got the boss drunk?" she blurted out, with a scowl that was tempered by an upward curve of her lips.

"Not likely!" I said. "If he was drunk, he got himself that way!"

She smiled. "I think I'd like a glass of wine, if your offer is still good." I'd promised her lunch, not wine, but she was there and that was the important thing.

We sat down at one of the tables and Eddie quit twisting lemon peel long enough to wait on us. I ordered black coffee, while Carol asked for a glass of Chardonnay. She had only a couple of sips, then we headed for the restaurant, leaving her half-empty glass.

Walking across the square, the sun burned down from straight overhead. There wasn't a breath of air, and we weren't halfway across before I was sweating like a nervous horse. I was headed for the Mexican place, but Carol took my arm to guide me on past it.

"Where're we going?" I wanted to know.

"Ma Hanrahan's. It's the best food in town."

Still clutching my arm, I let her lead. I only wanted to get out of the heat. She looked cool enough in her sleeveless dress. The starch was still stiff and clean around her carefully ironed collar. My own collar was wet and felt crumpled on the back of my neck, while perspiration seeped through the cloth covering my back.

Ma Hanrahan's was two blocks off the square, the last business place on the street before the residential tracts. It was on a corner directly across from a two-story red-brick house.

Ma's was situated in a small frame building with two big plate-glass windows in front and the door wedged between them. The windows had been painted black almost to eye level and then edged with a thin stripe of *Ma Hanrahan*, which was emblazoned in red on each of the windows. Printed in Old English script, the red contrasted sharply against the black.

It wasn't fancy, but it looked clean. The walls and ceiling were painted a light blue and about halfway up the wall was a red strip the same width as the one topping the black on the front windows. It ran clear around the room, interrupted only by a clock and two ancient Coca-Cola signs.

A long counter with low stools extended along one side of the room, while the opposite wall was crowded with a row of booths built of what looked like white pine and heavy plywood. They had been stained a deep mahogany. A jukebox hunkered against the back wall beneath the electric clock. It was an old machine with none of the colored lights and tubes of bubbling fluids that lit up the hotel bar.

There was no one in the place, but under the swinging doors at the end of the counter, I could see a woman's legs.

She came out of the kitchen heading toward us. Her friendly smile showed two gold teeth and deep wrinkles around the corners of her eyes and mouth. Her long hair was wrapped around the top of her head in a braided crown.

"What've you got today, Ma?" Carol asked, as we slid into one of the booths near the back.

"Depends. Want it hot or cold?" Her voice was deep and clear, almost a man's.

"Cold, I guess. It's too hot for anything else."

"How about cold ham and potato salad? Maybe some iced tea with it."

Carol nodded. "That's good for me. How about you?"

I nodded in agreement.

It didn't take long for her to bring the two plates, and while we waited we played the jukebox. I put in a couple of dollars worth of quarters and it played all the time we were eating. I paid the bill, breaking a twenty. It was part of the advance Riggson had given me the day before, and I still hadn't done anything about earning it. I wondered if I was on the payroll while I was waiting for things to start moving again. Not likely.

As Carol and I walked back to the office, she told me a little about what there was to do for entertainment in the town. On a side street was a theater that played only Spanish-language features for the local Latinos. Carol told me she went to see a film there once, though she didn't speak any Spanish. "Just a change of pace, in a town that never changes," she said with a far-away voice.

Leaving Carol at the office after doing my gentleman act and unlocking the door for her, I walked slowly up the sidewalk to the hotel. I paused to check the thermometer on the north corner of the building and wished I hadn't. It registered a hundred eighteen degrees. The clerk wasn't at the desk, but I had my room key in my pocket.

The second floor hallway was cool for the first time since I'd been there. The windows at each end of the corridor were down, and I could hear the hum of the air-conditioning system somewhere nearby.

Without thinking about the key, I twisted the knob. It turned in my hand and I paused, suddenly conscious. I know I had locked it that morning when I had left. I distinctly remembered turning the lock and pocketing the key.

I turned the knob cautiously until it stopped, then inched the door open. The door squeaked on its hinges, and I heard a sudden rustling inside. I kicked it open wide.

The housekeeper stood there for long seconds, hunched over my open suitcase. Her mouth was open with surprise and there was something I couldn't interpret in her eyes.

The clothing was ruffled and messed up, and the corner of an envelope containing my Marine Corps separation papers protruded from the mess. None of this bothered me nearly so much as the fact that my automatic was clutched loosely in her fingers.

Chapter Seven

The young woman stood there, staring at me with surprised eyes. I kept watching the pistol that hung limply in her hand. I expected those fingers to tighten and to find the gun pointed at me. Beyond that, I didn't think. I didn't want to.

"I was putting your clothes away, señor." Her English was careful and precise. She dropped the weapon back in the open suitcase and straightened up. "Señor Maxwell said you are staying for a time. I was going to put your clothes in the dresser and leave the suitcase in the closet."

"Who's Maxwell?" I almost yelled the question.

"The desk clerk, Señor Maxwell."

I'd never heard the man's name before, and it seemed strange that a little, dried-up hunk of humanity like him would be named Maxwell. For some reason I've never figured out, I always associate that name with a he-man. It's like thinking of the Great John L. when you hear the name Sullivan.

"Go ahead." I nodded. "Put the stuff away."

I sat down on the bed and lit a cigarette, staring at her,

watching her every move. Facing the girl with the gun in her hand had sent ripples of fear coursing up and down my spine.

I watched her put away the clothes, taking each piece out of the bag and stacking it neatly into a drawer. In retrospect, I should have taken the gun out of the bag, but she didn't pick it up again. With the clothing stowed, all that was left in the bottom of the suitcase was the gun and the big brown envelope holding my personal papers. She looked down at them, then at me.

"What do you want done with these, señor?"

"I'll take care of them. Don't ever touch the gun again."

She turned at the door and paused. "Is there anything else?" I looked at her carefully, searching her face. I wasn't certain what she meant. The surprise and fright were gone. There was no expression at all from which I could make a judgment. I shook my head.

I locked the door after she went out, kicked my shoes off, then hung my sticky shirt over a chair before I crawled back on the bed. I lay there, staring at the ceiling and wondering what I should do with the pistol. I could lock it in the suitcase and put it in the closet or leave it in the drawer with my clothes. I could leave it under my pillow, too, but the housekeeping maid would have a chance to fool with it every time she made the bed. She might accidentally shoot herself!

I slid off the bed and picked the .45 auto out of the open suitcase. It was old, but a good shooter. I slid the magazine out of the butt, then, one by one, I thumbed the cartridges out into my hand, counting them. They were all there. After looking the pistol over and testing it, I reloaded the clip and slid it back into the butt. It hadn't been tampered with as nearly as I could tell.

I parked it on top of the brown envelope and went back to sit on the bed. I looked through all of my pockets without finding a cigarette, then started to look through the pockets in the suitcase before I remembered I had pulled out my last extra pack the day before, when I'd been standing outside of Yuma, waiting for a ride.

I locked the door behind me and went down the stairs. I was headed for the bar when the clerk spoke to me from behind his desk.

"What'd you do to that room maid, feller?" He was scowling at me over the top of his glasses.

"What do you mean?"

"She came down them stairs as scared and mad as I ever seen a woman in my life."

"I caught her going through the stuff in my suitcase," I said. "All I did was let her know that I didn't like it." I decided it was best not to mention the gun.

"She wasn't doin' nothin' wrong. I told her to put away your stuff while she was cleanin' up."

"I'll put my own stuff away from now on. I don't need people pawing through it."

Still scowling, he shrugged and turned his attention to his papers.

The sheriff was mounted on a stool at the end of the bar, flipping the pages of a magazine, a half-finished draft beer in front of him. The barman was engrossed in his favorite pastime of stripping the skin off lemons and twisting the pieces into peculiar shapes.

I slid onto the stool next to the sheriff and motioned to

the bartender, who looked up without interrupting his citrus-peeling process.

''Plain Coke, again?'' he asked, looking critically at the knife blade, then the half-peeled lemon.

''I'll settle for that.'' I looked at the sheriff, engrossed in his copy of *True Police Cases*. ''Want another beer, Barney?''

''Nope.'' He tipped his glass, glancing at the foam marks. ''I got work to do.''

I remembered then that cigarettes were really what I'd come after. The bartender slid the filled Coke glass in front of me.

''Better bring me a pack of Luckies, too.'' I turned back to the sheriff. I knew I was going to take him by surprise, and I savored putting him on the spot.

''How come you took that old prospector's finger-prints?'' I was watching the sheriff and his expression didn't change. He tipped his beer glass and sloshed the white foam up the sides.

''Somebody's been serving you too much caffeine, boy. Nobody's taken prints on Hickory.'' He stared at me, cocking his head to one side. ''Where'd you get a fool idea like that?''

I didn't know what to say then. The surprise I'd been expecting wasn't there. As a matter of fact, the lawman looked almost bored—bored and a little amused.

I tore open the pack of cigarettes the bartender pushed at me. Then I noticed the sheriff wasn't interested in his magazine anymore. He sat there, twisting his beer glass and waiting for me to answer his question. The quick, jerky movements of his fingers rotating the glass reflected his nervousness, and I went ahead and lit my cigarette before I answered.

"Maybe you didn't fingerprint him, but somebody did." I inhaled a long drag and let it drift out my nostrils. "I saw ink on his fingers when Riggson and I hung in after the inquest."

The sheriff grinned and pushed his empty glass away. "Playin' detective, huh?"

I didn't like the slitted eyes. It was the kind of look a carpenter might give his son if he caught him cutting a brick in half with his favorite saw.

"I just noticed it," I said. "You can't blame me for wondering."

"I don't think Jeff had anything to do with it. Marks probably took them. No one knows much about the old guy, and the undertaker'd want sure identification for his files." Gould slid off the stool and tucked his detective magazine in the hip pocket of his trousers. "I'll check with him, but I think you was seein' things."

The thing about Marks taking the prints sounded pretty lame, and the way Gould had said it made it even less likely. Spur-of-the-moment thinking; there had been an odd note in his voice that made me certain he hadn't believed it himself.

Maxwell was stuffing mail into the different boxes as I sauntered into the lobby. He saw me and held out a plain white envelope as I passed, headed for the stairs.

"Somebody knows you're stoppin' here. San Francisco postmark."

I glanced at him as I took the envelope, but his back was turned and he was sorting more envelopes. One big stack stood on the counter.

''Don't know why Riggson can't have his mail sent to his office 'stead of here,'' Maxwell muttered, adding another envelope to the big pile.

I knew who my letter was from even before I opened it. Ferguson was the only person who would have written. Reaching my room, I lit up a cigarette, noting the envelope was addressed in ink, but the letter was typewritten on copy paper.

Dear Sam,

Enclosed you'll find a clipping on your first story about your own personal little murder situation—it's not exactly the way you gave it to me on the phone, since we had to put a rewrite man on it. You'll also find enclosed a check for $50. That comes out of your pay when you get on regular salary, so don't get the idea that you're getting money like that every time you turn in a few lines.

You've been in the newspaper biz long enough to know the entire state of California is not going to be interested in some insignificant village murder. I want you to keep playing up this angle about the Spanish treasure ship— that's the thing that'll arouse curiosity and keep people interested enough to buy newspapers. Mystery and missing treasure are sure things. Of course, having a murder tied in doesn't hurt.

I'm not telling you how to write your stories, Sam. I'm just making a couple of points that you can probably use.

An ardent fan—
Johhny

I liked the closing just above the scrawled name. That was the way Johnny had always been. Kidding me into thinking I was better than I was, laughingly playing hero-worshiper, when all the time he knew he was as good a newspaper man as there was on the West Coast.

His problem was frustration. He wanted to do the same things I had—drifting around, playing at being a hobo, studying people. He'd admitted to me once that those were things he would have liked to do, too. But a wife and three kids had kept him plugging along at newspaper work, leaving a job only when there was the promise of a better one. Johnny'd gotten to be an editor with his move to San Francisco. No hick sheets for him, only the big time.

I thought of the three dollars and change I'd had when I'd landed in Beale. If I told him about that, he might not feel so envious. Johnny had always liked to eat well. He'd order steak when the rest of us grabbed sandwiches on the run. He wouldn't have seen anything glamorous or adventurous about trying to exist on three bucks.

I folded the check and tucked it in a corner of my wallet. No telling when I'd get a chance to cash it. If I tried it at the local bank, everyone in town soon would know I was getting checks from a newspaper.

As for the letter, the tone of it told me Ferguson had passed a copy to someone higher on the corporate totem. He probably had had a tough time selling a series idea by a man none of them knew. The fact that he had fed my own ideas back to me told me what was happening.

I tore up the letter, dropped it in the ashtray, then touched the ash of my cigarette to a ragged corner of one of the particles. The little pile smoldered for a second or so before flaming and melting into a mound of crispy black. I was still staring at the ashes when there was a knock at the door.

''Yes?'' I supposed it was the maid again, but it wasn't.

It was the night bar waitress. She opened the door slowly and looked around the room before she came in.

"If we're going to be neighbors we might as well meet," she said. "I live next door."

"Come on in."

She was smiling and there was no trace of the hatred I'd seen on her face the night before. She leaned against the door for a second, letting me look her over. Green slacks, matching green silk polka-dotted blouse. Her hair was still bleached and dead looking, but she wasn't wearing the heavy makeup of the night before. She favored bright lipstick and had a healthy suntan on her face and arms.

She shut the door and came into the room. I motioned to one of the chairs and she nodded as she moved over to it and sat down. She didn't say anything say anything until she'd pulled up one leg of her slacks, and her nails were painted the exact shade as her lipstick. I noted that her ankles and what I could see of her legs were an even darker tan than her face. What appeared at first to be green eyes carried little flecks of gray and made them an in-between color. First she glanced at the open suitcase there in the middle of the floor, the .45 auto on full display. Then her eyes locked in on me.

"You're Sam Light. I know that," she said, looking at me curiously. "I'm Teala Locket."

"I saw you last night in the bar," I told her.

She nodded. "I'm flattered. Most people think barmaids are part of the furniture."

That was, I suppose, my cue to tell her she was different. I didn't.

"This is the hottest country I've ever been in. How do you go about keeping cool?" It was cool enough in the room, but I was looking out the window at the deserted, sun-stricken street.

She laughed. "We took a hint from the Mexicans. During the summer, a siesta's the thing. This town all but closes up for a couple of hours every afternoon."

I was surprised at the way she talked. Her diction was careful and proper, and I wondered whether she wasn't trying to make an impression. There was something a little too refined. It reminded me of the time I'd gone bar-hopping with an old friend I'd worked with until he'd gotten Hollywood fever and started writing for network television.

We'd been sitting in a little place out on Sunset Boulevard drinking and talking when a girl came over and invited him to dance. She and that super-refined voice of hers had been with us the rest of the evening. I'd heard from this guy later on and gotten the rest of it. The girl had recognized him as a film writer. The refinement was just a front for a stenographer from Kansas City who wanted a Hollywood career. Now I couldn't help wondering what Teala Locket was after.

"I could call down for a something cold," I offered, but she shook her head.

"If you did, I'd have to go after them. They haven't learned about room service here. Besides, I have to catch a nap. I sleep a little every afternoon to be able to keep the night hours I work. Then I'm supposed to have dinner with Jeff Street."

"What time do you go on?"

"I work the six to one A.M. shift, but it's always after two before we get done cleaning up the bar."

"Yeah." I nodded. "I used to tend bar."

"Oh?" She made the one syllable a question. "Where was that?"

"Miami. A place called the Buckhorn."

She shook her head. "I've never been to Miami." She stood up. "Well, I thought since we're next-door neighbors and both working for Riggson, we might as well get acquainted."

"Yeah. I'll probably see you tonight."

After she left, I dropped back on the bed and closed my eyes. I felt dead, and I was thankful she hadn't stayed any longer.

I awoke with a start, and when I opened my eyes it was dark. I tried to remember going to sleep, but I couldn't. People never remember drifting off, I guess. It just creeps up on us.

I lay there trying to stretch the wrinkles out of my mind and find some semblance of order. I'd had a dream, but it didn't make much sense.

Old Hickory Taite had been lying on his slab over in the basement in the furniture store. That had been the beginning of the dream. Someone whose face I couldn't see had come into the room and had gone over to Hickory's resting place and pulled the sheet back. What happened then hadn't surprised me at all. It had seemed as natural as the sun setting at night—just one of those things that is supposed to happen. That was how it seemed in my dream.

The old prospector had sat up on the edge of his granite slab to face the person whose features seemed always to be in a shadow. Taite cooperated with the person taking his fingerprints, and when it was done, he wiped part of the ink off on the white sheet, lay back down, and allowed the person to pull the sheet over him again.

It all came back to the point that had been bothering me all day. Someone had taken the old fellow's fingerprints. There was something important connected with that. I was sure of it. But what? The sheriff insisted he knew nothing about it, yet his nervousness had shown concern.

There was a sound outside my window. It was dark in the room, but the window was outlined by the reflected lights from the street below. The sound came again, and I could see a crouched figure silhouetted. My window was nearly half open. I saw that before I heard the choked breathing, then saw the silvery glint of gun metal.

My own gun was still in the middle of the floor in my open suitcase. Without really realizing I was sweating, I started to wipe the water off my forehead. I stopped before I started. Any sudden movement or shifting of my weight might lead the man at the window to start shooting.

The window went up a little more, making the same slight shriek as before, and the figure straightened a little. Then came the shot, and I dived for the suitcase lying there in the middle of the floor. Or maybe I made the plunge before the shot.

Chapter Eight

There was a shot, but no flame came out of the gun's muzzle. An instant later, I knew why. The figure at the window stiffened, then stumbled backward. I heard the splintering of the wooden porch rail and saw the thin, dark figure plunge backward and down. The expected thud and rattle of gravel followed, as the body hit the street.

My hand found the .45 Colt and I crouched there behind my suitcase, waiting. I felt foolish, using a cheap cardboard suitcase as a shield, but there was nothing else.

"Sam! Sam Light!" The voice was low and muffled, yet reflecting urgency. I didn't answer. Instead, I pulled back the slide on the automatic and allowed it to slam forward, pushing a cartridge into the chamber. There in the small room, the sliding metal sounded like the clash of gears in a tractor.

"You okay, Sam? It's Chet Riggson." The voice was right outside my window now, and I recognized it. Riggson still didn't show himself.

"I'm okay, I guess."

"You got a gun?"

"You'd better know it!" My hand was tight on the grip, finger on the trigger.

"Don't shoot. I'm comin' in."

He pushed the window all the way to the top, then wriggled his bulk through the opening. I saw him straighten to his full stature in the dimness.

"We'd better leave the light off. There's going to be a crowd down there, and we don't need them up here," Riggson said. I could see the glint of the long-barreled six-gun he was still holding.

"What's this all about?" I demanded. The sweat was streaming down my face, and for the first time I had a chance to wipe it off on my sleeve.

"I don't know. I couldn't tell who it was. Too dark."

"But why?" I insisted. There were people in the street under my window now and I could hear the bubbling sound of excited voices.

"I don't know that, either. Remember the story about the narcotics agent who got knocked off?"

"I'm no government man!"

"I believe you, but there's no reason other people should. You've been right in the thick of things ever since you hit here."

What he said made sense. I'd happened in right in the middle of a murder, and anyone could see easily enough that I was being way too nosy. I swore silently at myself for mentioning the ink I'd seen on the old prospector's hands. I should have kept my mouth shut, even to the sheriff.

"We'd better get down there, Light. Barney Gould's probably tryin' to pin this on somebody already."

It was dark in the side street, but there were probably a

couple of dozen people—late drinkers from the hotel bar, I assumed—gathered in a tight knot. Riggson pushed through to where Gould and Jeff Street were bending over the body with flashlights.

"He dead?" Riggson asked.

"Deader'n buzzard bait." The sheriff looked up, while I stared down at the huddled body on the ground. It was Maxwell, the desk clerk. The sheriff was right about him being dead.

"I shot him, Sheriff. I'm responsible." Riggson made it a statement of fact.

The sheriff centered the rays from the flashlight full in the big man's face. Riggson blinked and stepped back as both officers stood up from the body.

"Why'd you shoot him?" the deputy demanded.

"Hadn't we better find a better place to talk it over?"

The voices of the onlookers, some of them half drunk but still in shock, had died, and everyone was standing there, staring at Riggson, the sheriff, and myself. Gould looked around at the faces before answering.

"We'd better get over to the office." He glanced at his deputy. "Jeff, get Doc Blanch over here to look at this guy b'fore we move him. Get the undertaker, too.

"Let's go, Chet." The crowd parted for him as he started toward the jail. "You'd better come along, too, Light. I'll want to talk to you."

I could hear Jeff Street directing someone to call the doctor and someone else to find Marks, the undertaker, as we walked across the street toward the solid brick building where I'd spent several hours the afternoon before.

All of the events of the past two days were taking on an air of the totally bizarre. Riggson had come to my rescue

yesterday, and his testimony had been the cause of my release. Now they were going to lock him up and maybe I'd
be called to testify for him. That had to come under the
heading of one of the lesser types of poetic justice!

It was almost the same as it had been with me. Riggson
sat in the chair across the desk from the sheriff. I stood and
looked out the window as Riggson had the afternoon before, when they'd been questioning me.

"Wanna tell me what this is all about, Chet, or d'you
want a lawyer? Shootin' people's a Death Row offense."

"I don't need any fool lawyer!"

Gould leaned back in his chair and rested one boot on
the edge of his desk, careful not to disturb any of the papers
that covered its surface. He was taking this killing just as
nonchalantly as he had the murder of Hickory Taite.

"Go ahead." He nodded. "Let's have it."

"There's not much to tell. I went up to my room about
eleven-thirty and was lyin' on my bed, thinking, when I
heard someone walking around on the sundeck outside my
window."

Riggson elaborated on what he had told me. He explained quietly that he'd seen a figure sneak past his window with a gun in his hand, and how he'd watched the
person, who had turned out to be Maxwell, getting ready
to shoot me.

The sheriff frowned for a moment, eyes narrowed, glancing from one of us to the other. "Why aren't there any
screens on those windows, Chet?"

Riggson offered a shrug. "I had 'em all pulled off and
sent down to Calexico to be rescreened. They were rusted
out."

Nodding acceptance of the explanation, Barney Gould

reached into his pocket and drew out a faded bandanna. He spread the handkerchief out on the top of his desk, looking at the pistol it had covered.

"This the gun Maxwell was carryin'? Thirty-two caliber. Smith & Wesson."

Riggson shook his head. "I didn't get that good a look at it. I didn't recognize Maxwell, let alone his gun."

Gould picked up the revolver, using a pencil through the trigger guard. "This must be it. We found it right near the body." He turned and looked at me.

"What've you got to say about this, Light? This is the second killin' you've been in on in two days." His tone was good-natured, but I didn't care for his comment at all.

"I had fallen asleep, but I woke up to see somebody trying to open my window. I could see he was carrying a gun."

"This gun?" He pointed at the .32 Smith & Wesson suspended on his pencil.

I shook my head. "It was too dark to tell what it looked like. I just saw a reflection in the light from the street."

"Was Maxwell about to fire when Riggson shot him?"

I had to shake my head again. "I don't know for sure. I'm a little confused. I was trying to get to my own gun." I thought of Maxwell sending the maid up to put my stuff away and finding her playing with my automatic, but it seemed best not to mention it to Gould. I'd said too much when I'd told him about the ink on the fingers of the corpse. I'd seen something, too, when I'd been looking at the pistol lying there on the bandanna. The corner of a card was sticking out from under the other papers on the desk. It was sticking out just far enough for me to see part of a black fingerprint inked on the paper. It couldn't belong to anyone except Hickory Taite. Who else would Gould or Jeff have fingerprinted?

The sheriff stood up and wrapped the pistol in the bandanna again.

"You tell a straight story, Chet, but it wouldn't be too hard to slap a manslaughter charge on you if someone really wanted to."

Riggson's next word was spelled with four letters before he added, "Why'd anyone do that? I reacted the way most anyone else would. And I probably saved Sam from gettin' killed!"

Gould put the wrapped weapon in a desk drawer and locked it before he answered with a shake of his head. "Can't tell much about the law or what it's goin' to do anymore, Chet. Just read about a case over in Arizona. Feller saw a guy goin' into his chicken house at night and shot into it with buckshot. They ran him in for manslaughter, even though there was a whole sackful of chickens right there beside the body. Looks to me like this's pretty much the same thing. You got Light here, of course, and Maxwell had a gun instead of a sack of chickens."

Riggson growled a curse as he stood up, leaning across the desk toward the sheriff, eyes narrowed. "Maybe I do need a lawyer."

"Not now. I'm goin' to turn you loose for the time bein' on your own recognizance, Chet." Gould moved out from behind the desk and motioned toward the door. "I'm considerin' it justifiable homicide until tomorrow. There'll have to be an inquest. Both of you'll have to be there, again."

"This is getting to be a daily affair," Riggson grumbled, scowling, but the sheriff's decision had calmed him a bit.

Gould herded us back into the street and pulled the office door shut behind him. Over at the hotel there were still little groups of people standing about, undoubtedly discussing the new turn of events. Others were in front of the mortuary/furniture store up the street. There were a lot more people up and about at 1:30 in the morning.

"Guess they got him on a slab by now," Gould said. "Either one of you comin' up there with me?"

I waited for Riggson to answer and watched as he shook his head.

"I've seen enough, Barney. Maxwell never done anything to me, and I probably won't sleep tonight." He spoke slowly and his head was down and shadowed so I couldn't see his face. It rather surprised me. I'd never seen that side of Riggson before—the soft side. He'd impressed me as being efficient and honestly ruthless.

"That's me, too, Sheriff. I feel about the same way," I said.

Gould stared at me and shook his head slowly. I expected him to give me that slow, knowing grin, but he didn't.

"Guy tries to shoot you and you wish he hadn't been killed. That's not exactly what I'd call an eye-for-an-eye doctrine. What are you? One of them turn-the-other-cheek believers? Any idea why he was after you?"

He stared at me for another moment, then turned and walked away. I stood watching his back as he lumbered up the street toward the furniture store, where Marks, the mortician, undoubtedly had Maxwell's body spread out on a slab beside that of Hickory Taite.

There had been more than a note of sarcasm in the sheriff's voice, and it disturbed me to realize I did feel an odd kind of guilt. I was the reason the little hotel clerk had been killed, even if I hadn't shot him.

I'd started planning as soon as I'd seen the fingerprints on Gould's desk, so I went back to the hotel with Riggson. He went behind the registration desk and turned on a light, looking around. Neither of us spoke as I climbed the stairs to my room, wondering who would be watching the desk in the morning. I turned on the light and put down the window, standing in front of it to take off my shirt. Anyone watching would think I was going to bed.

I turned off my light and stuffed my shirttail back in my pants before I went out, leaving the door unlocked, and tiptoed down the back stairway leading to the alley.

I followed the alley for two blocks, careful to keep to the shadows. Gould denied knowing anything about the fingerprints, yet they were on his desk. I wanted a copy of them, and if whoever had taken them knew anything at all about police procedure, there were certain to be several sets. Mixed in with these thoughts was the question of what Gould and Street had been doing in the vicinity of the hotel after midnight. They could have been in the bar, of course.

I kept to the alleys and out of the streetlights as much as I could until I was directly behind the jail. I edged along the side of the building until I was at the corner near the door. I had noted when we left that the sheriff had not locked it. Trust is strong in small towns, and he was coming back.

I looked up and down the street. It was empty, although there was a light on in the furniture store. Gould would still be there. Luckily, one of the palm trees in the square slanted a long shadow that left the front of the sheriff's office in near darkness.

The door swung open easily and I was careful to close it behind me. I stood listening for a second, but the only sound was the chirping of a cricket back toward the cell block. I groped my way along the wall until I was in the sheriff's office. I struck a match then and moved to the desk, careful to shade the flame with my hand.

I didn't even have to dig through the other papers on Gould's desk. One corner of the fingerprint card was visible just as I'd noted earlier. There were three more copies underneath it, and I took the one off the bottom. I wanted everything on the desk to appear just as it had been when Gould left.

I stuck the card inside my shirt and put out the match. I had the fingerprints with Hickory Taite's name on the top of the card. I knew what my next move had to be.

Chapter Nine

Once back in my room, I took off my shirt and turned on the light again. I hoped that if anyone had been spying on my room, they'd think I had been napping. I was certain no one had followed me to or from the sheriff's office. I'd been watching all of the time.

I sat down on the edge of my bed and looked at my take. Only one of the fingerprints was smudged, and it was still in good enough shape to be filed. I turned the card over. On the other side was Taite's name with the Hickory in quotation marks. Under that was a description that was no more original than any other police report I ever read. He had been five feet eight inches tall, weighed one hundred fifty-one pounds, had gray hair, a beard, and black eyes. That was all.

My suitcase was still lying in the middle of the floor where it had been when I'd made that frightened dive for my pistol an hour or so earlier. The .45 Colt was there, too, along with the envelope holding my papers.

Sticking from beneath the envelope was the clipping Ferguson had sent me concerning Taite's death. I'd forgotten I'd put it there.

In the bottom of the bag I found what I needed: a plain, stamped envelope. I wrote Johnny Ferguson's name and home address on the front of it, then folded the card in such a fashion that the fingerprints wouldn't be cracked.

I didn't want anyone around town, including the postmaster, connecting me with Johnny's paper, so there was no return address. It would come out sometime, but I wanted to maintain my hobo role as long as I could. I was more or less on the inside, and I'd get more of the details than I would as a reporter for the San Francisco *Citizen*. When there's trouble, most people don't want to talk to outsiders—not the way they gossip with people they know.

I went downstairs and dropped the envelope into the mailbox stationed near the desk. No one was there. Apparently Riggson hadn't thought about his hotel going unattended. Either that or he hadn't gotten around to getting somebody to serve as clerk. I thought of offering my services.

I used the pay phone and got long distance after some trouble. It was almost 3:00 when the operator told Johnny he had a collect call from me.

"What's the idea of calling collect? That fifty bucks I sent wasn't just for wild, riotous living, you know." He had been asleep, of course, and had a right to be grumpy. He reminded me of a sideshow barker giving his last spiel of the day. A little tired, totally bored, and in a hurry to get done.

"Finished?" I asked.

"What d'you want?"

"There's been an attempted murder down here, plus another killing," I said. "Both in this same hotel, too."

I paused for a second, but Johnny didn't say anything. He waited.

"This time the intended victim was some hobo named Sam Light."

"What the—Sam! What happened?" Ferguson was fully awake and his tone suggested he might be worried over my well-being. More likely he was contemplating how large a headline he should put on the story.

"I'm not real sure what it was all about. I was asleep, when the hotel clerk tried to come through the window with a pistol in his hand. He got shot for his trouble."

"You shoot him?"

"No. The man who owns the hotel saw him sneaking toward my window with a gun in his hand. When the guy got my window up and pointed the darn thing at me, Chet Riggson stepped in with a gun of his own."

"Sheesh!" It was almost a groan. Johnny couldn't have reporters who weren't even on the regular payroll getting themselves shot up.

"You getting all this down on paper?" I asked. For years, Ferguson had slept with a pad and copy pencil beside his phone. He ignored my question.

"Give me the names of the people involved and I'll turn it over to rewrite. With luck, we can get into the early edition."

I gave him Maxwell's name, along with Riggson's, that of Sheriff Gould and Jeff Street, then quickly told him where they fitted in.

"Okay. I've got it. I'm going to leave you out of it as anything other than a near victim. This piece'll be strictly third person by one of the rewrite men. That way maybe no one will connect you with us. Not yet, at least.''

''That's why I call collect. If I cash your check here, everyone in town will know I'm working on this.''

I hadn't seen a San Francisco newspaper since I'd gotten into town, although I'd spotted several Los Angeles sheets on a stand at the drugstore across the square. If no one knew I was a reporter for the paper and no one read the paper anyhow, I'd hear more.

''There's a little thing coming to your home address about tomorrow afternoon that I need further info on. You can get one of your cop friends to check it out. You've been in town long enough to have that much influence.''

''What is it?''

''You'll see when it gets there. I'm talking too much right now.''

''Oh?'' he said. ''Walls with ears?''

''Maybe. If anything new comes up, I'll let you know.''

''Okay. I'm knocking off. This call's costing money.''

''You should worry.'' My retort was cut off by the distant click followed by a dial tone.

I was pushing open the door of the phone booth when Carol came in the front lobby door. She took a heavy drag off the cigarette she was smoking and dropped it in the brass spittoon standing against the door sill. It was then that she saw me and frowned.

''Aren't you back in bed yet?''

I shook my head. ''Haven't felt much like sleeping after what happened.'' I tried to sound nonchalant and at ease. I think I sounded convincing.

''I heard about it. Chet's call woke me up. He told me.''

''Where're you going now?'' I was a little disappointed.

I wanted her to ask me more about what had happened. I'd thought she'd want to hear about it from me, even if everyone else in town had already told her.

"Nowhere." She shook her head. "I'm supposed to sit here and fill in for a corpse." The words were flippant, but her lips twisted in a grimace of distaste.

"Maxwell, you mean? That doesn't allow you much sleep."

"I'll sit in one of those and nap." She pointed to a pair of overstuffed armchairs. "There won't be anyone checking in here tonight."

Barney Gould invaded my thoughts while I was talking to her. Her crack about filling in for a corpse was what did it. Maxwell's death seemingly meant nothing to her, and she tended to shrug it off just as Gould had done in the case of both Maxwell and Hickory Taite.

All along, Gould's attitude had been that they were simply dead. Nothing was actually lost, but it still was up to him to make an official investigation and get it over with as soon as, and as neatly as, possible. Maybe all the people in town had that attitude.

Carol took another cigarette out of her purse and lit it. She blew a cloud of smoke at the ceiling, then looked at me again, seeming to study my face for a moment.

"Sam, why don't you get out of this town before you get killed?" Her eyes were narrowed and there was a slight frown on her face. It was like a movie advertisement I saw once plugging a character called the Panther Woman. I'd never seen this side of her before.

"Interested in my health?"

"Be serious. There's something going on I don't understand. No one does, unless it's you."

"I know even less than anyone else. I just got here." I shrugged. "Don't look at me."

"Someone's looking at you, or Maxwell wouldn't have tried to shoot you."

"Maybe they think I'm a narc agent like Riggson says."

It was her turn to shrug. "Maybe. There's always been dope coming across the border, and one or two agents more probably won't stop it."

She paused, then shook her head. "One thing I know. You're no hobo and you're no fruit tramp. Your hands are too smooth. Besides, all the picking's done by Mexicans these days."

It was well onto 4:00 when I finally got to bed. I checked that my windows were locked, then tucked the .45 Colt under my pillow. As I waited to doze off, I considered the warning from the girl downstairs at the desk. My pondering advanced to the expression of the movie Panther Woman and the look Carol had flashed me. That must have been when I dropped off to sleep.

Carol wore a different expression the next morning when she came pounding on my door.

"For heaven's sake, Sam, wake up! Wake up!" Her voice was frantic through the door. Sunlight was streaming in my window and I sat up on the edge of the bed, reaching for my trousers.

"I'm coming!" I shouted. "What's going on?"

"Hurry up, Sam. You have to get up!"

"I'm up!" I snarled a curse as I unlocked the door and flung it open.

"What now?"

"Gould's in the lobby fit to be tied. They found Petey Basquez."

Petey, it came to me, was the Mexican kid who was supposed to have stolen the set of silver-handled knives from Riggson.

"Where is he?"

"They found his body out near the Mud Pots." She didn't even pause for breath. "And someone broke into the sheriff's office last night. Stole some fingerprints and the gun Maxwell was carrying when he got killed."

I picked up her arm to stare at her wristwatch. It was almost 10:00. It had all been well planned. Hickory Taite had been buried at 9:00 and now his fingerprints were gone. Not just the ones I'd taken, but the other sets, too. I was willing to wager on that. And the Basquez kid had been killed. I knew he'd been slain, even though Carol hadn't said so.

Chapter Ten

No one said anything until we were on the way to the Mud Pots. The sheriff hadn't even spoken when I came down from my room. Instead, he turned and led the way out the door to a big black Buick. Jeff Street was behind the wheel, while Marks, the coroner, and Chet Riggson were in the backseat. I crawled in beside Street, squeezing against him to make room for Gould.

We were doing eighty when we hit the flat ribbon of highway at the edge of town, and the speedometer bobbed back and forth between ninety and the white numerals of the hundred mark as we moved north.

"You weren't at Taite's funeral this morning," Gould noted. I turned and looked at him, but his eyes were on the road. I looked at Marks and Riggson in the backseat, but both seemed to be staring at the floor.

"I didn't wake up until Carol came up and started pounding on my door. Was I supposed to be there? I didn't even know the man."

"Just checkin' things out. Someone sneaked into my office and made away with some papers." He didn't look at me even then. His eyes were still on the road ahead. His voice was flat and even, and I wondered if he was accusing me or just stating a fact.

"What kind of papers?"

"Them fingerprints you were so worried about. And they took the gun Charlie Maxwell was carryin'."

"Taite's fingerprints?"

He nodded. "I took them after he died, just like you thought." His voice was the same as before—flat and easy, almost conversational.

"Somebody took what he wanted, then turned on the electric fan to cause a mighty mess and make it look accidental. Pretty good trick," he conceded.

"I had to pick up stuff all over the room before I missed them prints. And I hadn't had time to write down the serial number on Maxwell's revolver."

The Salton Sea was like a long flat sheet of silver from the edge of town, but as we sped toward it, the surface faded into the blue reflection of the sky. The sun was baking bright, and the thermometer had to be in the high nineties. Yet a thin sheet of fog seemed to hang over the water, veiling the range of mountains on the other side of the saltwater. Above the mist out there on the west side, the peaks of the Santa Rosa Mountains stood out clear and dark.

"If this thing's been here since an earthquake long ago, why hasn't it dried up?" I asked. Riggson was the one who answered from the backseat.

"It used to be called the Salton Trough. Old Indian legends say it had plenty of water in it a couple of times, but it was dry in 1905, when the Colorado River went on a rampage and diverted to the trough. It's been there ever since. Originally, it was fed by desert rains in the winter and water comin' off the mountains.

"Any fish in it?" I asked.

"Back after World War Two, mullet were netted on a commercial basis, but irrigation from our own people and Mexico started to pollute it. DDT and some of the other chemicals. There's more salt comin' in all the time, too, from agricultural efforts. It'd probably dry up if it wasn't for irrigation water that flows into it. That adds to the problem, because with the water comes fertilizer, insecticides, and who knows what else."

"Both California senators have been trying to get funds to restore it," Street put in, "but nobody has much faith in that happening in our lifetime."

"It may turn into a sewer in our lifetime," Marks added with a touch of bitterness. "Birds are bein' poisoned, and fish and game people are goin' crazy over dead birds they pick up off the shoreline. It's a mess."

Straight across those Santa Rosa Mountains was San Diego. From there, it was only a few hundred miles to San Francisco. Sitting there among the now-silent foursome, I felt the San Francisco *Citizen's* city room was a long way off.

Obviously, someone else had suspected Gould of having Hickory Taite's fingerprints, but I had been the only one foolish enough tell him of my suspicions. Anyone at the inquest could have seen the ink on the hands of the corpse, however.

"Couple of varmint hunters found Basquez's body." The sheriff's announcement cut into my thoughts. "One of them called in on a cell phone."

"How do you know it's Basquez?" Riggson asked from the backseat.

"It's Petey, right enough," Gould declared. "The feller described him to a T."

"What is there to hunt out here?" I wanted to know, surveying the scrub brush and sand that edged the lake.

"Coyotes mostly," Jeff Street answered. "Several species of ducks nest around here, and the coyotes play tough with their eggs. It's open season on varmints year-round out here."

"When'd you hear about Basquez?" Marks wanted to know. "You didn't do nothing but yell over the phone."

"I called you, then Chet, as soon as I heard. Had a little more trouble getting Light here. The Kirby gal figured he hadn't had his proper beauty sleep." The sheriff glanced at me and offered a knowing grin. I gave him a duty smile in return, recalling the way Carol had been pounding on my door. I don't usually sleep that heavily.

"Why'd you have to get me out of bed to come out here?" I asked. "I never saw the Basquez kid alive, let alone dead."

"Not sure why I brought you along, Sam," the sheriff explained amiably. "But you knew all about them fingerprints, and it was your room Taite got killed in. And you're the one Maxwell was gonna take a shot at. I just don't wanna see you get mixed up in what's comin' down any deeper than you are. Besides, I enjoy your company"

"Watch it!" Jeff Street warned suddenly. Rubber screamed on sun-softened blacktop before gravel rattled against the fenders as we sped down a side road toward the still, blue water. Then we stopped.

It looked like a flat, plowed field, one that had been

plowed the fall before with winter rains flattening out the lumps and clods. Back away from the road, I saw columns of steam coming up out of the gray dirt. An old truck and two men stood nearby.

We didn't have to get out of the car to see the body. Petey Basquez's white cotton shirt stood out in stark relief against the dark, bare ground. It was at least a hundred yards away, and the white could have passed for a crumpled, water-soaked newspaper if we hadn't known what it was. As I opened the car door and stepped out. I glanced at the lake a half-mile away. It wasn't as blue as it had seemed from afar. It looked muddy and troubled. The mist that hid the foot of the mountains on the opposite shore seemed thicker than ever. I glanced at Gould and saw the troubled frown and tight-set lips, as he led the way across the field.

The two men were dressed in camouflage pants and loose jackets, hiking boots on their feet. Both were tall and dark beneath their billed camo caps. One looked as if he might be of Italian or Portuguese descent. The other one had red hair sticking out from under his cap, and his dark complexion had to be due primarily to the wind and sun.

''We seen the buzzards circling around over here yesterday,'' the Italian-looking one said, addressing the sheriff. ''I told Todd here we oughta see what they was after, but it was sundown and we wanted to get in position for coyote callin' before dark.''

''The buzzards were circlin' yesterday, you say?'' the sheriff asked.

The man nodded. ''Same as now.'' He pointed upward and we all looked to the sky. They looked like huge crows as they glided around and around in circles. They were hard to see against the sun, and we all had to shade our eyes. They seemed lazy and patient, swooping upward on a current of air, then gliding easily downward, seldom needing to move their wings.

"But what're you doing here now?" Jeff Street wanted to know. The redhead looked at him with distaste and waited for the other to answer.

"We was out here all night, callin' and shootin'."

"How many did you get?" the sheriff asked.

"Seven," the redhead announced. "Missed a couple we should've had." He nodded toward their battered vehicle. "They're over there in the truck. There'd probably have been more of him for you to look at had we looked last night," he said. He took one step forward and glanced at Jeff Street to see what the effect of his words would be. Gould was still looking upward into the sun, watching the circling buzzards. Jeff Street answered for him.

Gould took his hand away from his face and looked around at us. He didn't like this job. It was obvious from the way he sighed, then hunched his shoulders and started slowly across the mud flat, the rest of us following.

The Mud Pots, half a dozen of them, were gathered in a group that reminded me of a well-used hog wallow. The mud was loose, runny stuff, most of it a deep gray color, standing in pools. From the center of the pools bubbled the continuous geysers of steam I had noticed from the road. Shooting straight up for several feet, the streams of vapor faded and dried out in the hot wind. The smell of salt and sulfur was heavy on the morning breeze as we moved past the first of the holes. I had the feeling we were standing at the edge of an active volcano, and that could well be the case.

The body was half submerged in the largest of the mud-holes. It was nearly six feet across, and the entire surface bubbled as diligently as a teakettle, sending up its cloud of hot vapor. One arm and one leg were buried in the mud, and the other half of the body rested on what appeared to be semisolid ground.

"Completely dehydrated," Marks said. I was watching him as he bent over the body, inspecting it with professional curiosity. "Dried out like an Indio date."

His body shielded most of the corpse from my sight, but as he straightened up again, I saw the Mexican boy's face, and I felt the nausea tightening in my stomach again. The boy looked to be no more than sixteen. His black hair was thick with the dried mud and the hot stream had scalded the skin.

From the moment Carol had awakened me, I had known Petey Basquez had been murdered, but I hadn't expected to see it like this. The hand that extended from the mudhole held what had to be one of the long-bladed Mexican knives stolen from Chet Riggson. The first of the set of three had killed Hickory Taite. The other two were here. And it had to be murder again. No man I've ever known has been strong enough to drive a knife to the hilt into his own chest. He just can't swing hard enough for that kind of entry. I stared down at the body, and as the carved dragon-head handle of the third dagger reflected the blazing sun, I fancied that one of the turquoise eyes mounted in the silver head blinked at me.

It was hot there. I remembered the stench of death from the Iraqi desert and I knew I was going to be sick.

Chapter Eleven

The image of Petey Basquez's body dominated my thoughts as we started back to town. Jeff Street drove more slowly this time, and we seemed to be crawling along the straight, flat highway, even though the speedometer registered sixty.

A middle-aged Mexican had brought Marks's hearse out from town, and we stayed until the body had been loaded into the somber black vehicle and covered with a black sheet. Then we started back, the hearse somewhere behind us. The two coyote hunters had gone about their business, after telling Jeff Street where they could be located when needed.

Loading the body into the hearse had been bad. It was the first time I had run into something like that since the Gulf War. It's an experience no one is ever likely to grow used to.

I had glanced at Gould, who was carrying one corner of the stretcher and its grisly load to the hearse parked at the end of the road. His eyes were on the ground and I could see the little lines of annoyance starting at his nostrils and running down past the corners of his mouth.

I'd seen Riggson's face, too, and had I not felt sick myself, I would have laughed. I knew that he felt as badly as I did, but on a man as big as him it looked odd. His face was dead white, and his breath was coming in short noisy gasps, like he was trying to hurry and finish with each breath.

"This stuff is going to foul up things in this county plenty," Riggson said from the backseat. I turned my head enough to look at him, wondering if his stomach still felt as unsettled as mine. His composure had returned, and he was leaning back comfortably against the cushions. "You better find someone to blame this on pretty soon, Gould, or people'll be wondering why they elected you."

"I had someone," Gould told him, tone suddenly sullen. "We had Light here for the Taite murder, till you vouched for him."

"Somethin's at the bottom of all this, and it ain't Light. He's not been around this country long enough to know as much as whoever is at the foot of Hickory Taite's killing."

"You mean Hickory's talk about the old treasure ship? There must be a dozen books that mention that old fable. Half the history and mythology buffs in the country probably know about it. Been enough of 'em down here huntin' for it."

The two of them were carrying on as though I wasn't even there, so I just sat there, while Riggson and Gould argued over whether I could have had anything to do with the killings. It wasn't any fun.

"They keep killin' people around this town, I'm goin'

to be out of business. That's the point I started to make,'' Chet said. ''I have a big corporate agro outfit interested in startin' a large-scale farmin' project on land we're gettin' ready to irrigate. They find out every stranger that comes through town gets mixed up in a killin', they're not goin' to send their tenant farmers anywhere near this area.''

His tone was easy and kind of joking when he started the speech, but he wasn't pulling any punches at the end of it. He meant what he said.

''Our local folks're pretty nice people, Chet,'' the sheriff said. ''I don't think there's anyone we know who is mean enough to run around killin' people just so you won't be able to sell your wet-down sand.''

The reference to Riggson's irrigation project caused me to glance at him. He was grinning a little and the worry lines were gone from his face. I realized then that I also felt better.

Jeff glanced at his wristwatch as we swung the car onto the square and slowed down in front of the hotel.

''Almost noon, Barney. Want me to run you home for lunch?''

''Let me off here,'' Riggson spoke up. ''I have to relieve the girl on the hotel desk so she can eat.''

''Yeah. I'll go on home,'' the sheriff decided. ''How about it, Marks? Gonna leave Petey in the black wagon till after chow?''

''Nope. I wanna get him out of there. Wanna look at that knife, too. Try to figger out whether he killed himself or it's someone else's work.''

''What do you mean?'' I knew my tone was demanding. ''How could a guy punch a knife into himself that far and die without dropping the knife he's got in the other hand?''

''Very simple.'' The coroner's tone was one of professional superiority. ''There're numerous cases in which people have thrown themselves on knives, drivin' them in when they hit the ground. Hangin' on to the other knife would be natural. If you were dyin', wouldn't you be grabbin' for somethin'?''

Riggson and I got out of the Buick there in front of the hotel and watched as Jeff drove on down the street to let Marks out in front of his furniture store.

''Where you going to eat, Sam?''

''I don't know. Ma Hanrahan's, I guess. That's where I've been eating.''

Riggson nodded. ''Wait, and I'll send Carol out. She eats over there, too, doesn't she?''

It was my turn to nod, and I waited in the shade of the veranda, while he pushed through the front door.

Carol looked tired, and it was apparent she'd had no sleep in spite of her announced plan to nap in the big easy chair during the night. The light cotton dress she was wearing was wrinkled, and there was a blot of ink on the skirt. She saw me looking at it.

''Just call me sloppy. I dropped a bottle of ink and almost drowned myself. Even got it in my hair. See how straight it is?'' She grabbed a lock and held it out away from her face. It was still damp on the ends, and what curl she'd had was gone.

''What'd you have to do? Wash it?''

''Yeah.'' She groaned. ''I had to do it in the ladies' restroom. I couldn't find anyone to take over the desk so I could go home to do it.''

Deep circles under eyes were dark against the tan of her face.

"You'd better get some sleep this afternoon. You must be bushed," I told her, but she shook her head.

"It's not that bad. I get these circles around my eyes any time I miss a night's sleep. An old family trait. Every time my father would go off on a bender, he'd come home looking like he was wearing greasepaint rings on his face. A night's sleep, though, and you'd never know he'd been on an extended drunk."

We were walking across the square when I thought to ask her if she had planned on eating at Hanrahan's.

"I told you it's the best place in town. Not that there's much to choose from." The last sounded bitter and it surprised me. After being up all night and splashing ink in her hair, she'd been happy. But her evaluation regarding the size of the town had brought on that tinge of dislike. She caught me looking at her and laughed.

The menu at Ma Hanrahan's was pretty much the same as it had been the day before. In fact, I could see no difference. I asked Carol about it when we were settled in one of the booths.

"It's the same all week long except Fridays. She'll add some kind of fish to the menu today. Has to, with all the Mexicans and a lot of the other people around here being Catholic."

"I thought the Pope had eased up on that fish-on-Friday routine."

She shook her head. "You don't understand the people here, Sam. They're not much for change of the status quo. If it was good enough for their grandparents, it's good enough now." That tinge of unrest was back in her tone.

"This isn't the only place that sort of thinking goes on," I told her.

Suddenly serious, she leaned across the table, frowning. "What about Petey? I asked Chet, but he said you could tell me all about it at lunch."

"You pick a nice topic for mealtime discussion." I was remembering the unpleasant experience again.

"I'm sorry. I don't need to know." If anyone over the age of nine can pout, she was, and I hurried to explain.

"Actually, there's not much to tell. I don't know anything except what I saw out at the Mud Pots."

"I have a theory," she said, leaning close again. "I think the three of them were partners. Taite, Petey, and Maxwell."

"Partners in what?" The idea of a teenage Mexican being in partnership with the two Yank oldsters didn't make much sense.

"Smuggling drugs or maybe something else across the border. Taite was trying to double-cross the other two, so Petey killed him. Taite, with his prospecting cover, had the run of the country and would be in good position to double-cross the other two. Maxwell and Petey were pretty much stuck right here in town where they could keep an eye on each other. They wouldn't have much chance to sell out, but Taite would."

"Sell out what to whom?"

"Come on, Sam, be sensible! Everyone knows drugs come across the border around here. Millions of dollars every year. And any big operator'd like to get a corner on it."

"Go on. I'm listening."

"Well, it's reasonable that if Taite tried a double-cross, Basquez killed him with one of the knives he stole from

Chet.'' She stopped for a second, waiting to see if I was going to agree. When I didn't react, she continued.

''The kid knew Riggson would identify the knife, so he hid out there near the Mud Pots. He wouldn't be fool enough to try hitchhiking to either Los Angeles or the border. Something like this happens, the first thing Jeff and Gould do is notify the Border Patrol and other law enforcement agencies.

''Out there alone in the desert, Petey must have decided on suicide. Realizing he probably was wanted for murder and having that sun beating down on his bare head all day would drive anyone to suicide. It must have been that.''

''What about Maxwell?''

''That's the simplest part of it all,'' she said. She was leaning very close across the table now, and I realized her hair had dried and the curl had reappeared in the ends of the dark locks.

''Maxwell suspected every stranger who stayed in town more than a few hours of being a government narc, and the way you got mixed up in this thing, he picked you out as dangerous. Maybe the fact that he hadn't heard from Petey Basquez was bothering him. You being right there in the hotel where you could watch his moves was enough to scare him into trying to kill you. If it hadn't been for Chet, he'd have gotten you.''

She sat there, waiting for me to say something. She wouldn't like it when I did, so I took my cigarettes out of my shirt pocket and offered her one. She offered an impatient shake of her head. I lit mine. Leaning back in the booth, I blew a smoke ring in the air and watched it dissolve before I spoke.

''You've been reading too many detective novels. A couple of books on psychology would show you people are basically interested in their own welfare. They just don't run around stabbing people, then committing suicide to cover it up. They certainly don't gain anything by it. Getting dead is not to the individual's benefit, and he won't do it."

She started to say something as I took another drag off my cigarette, but I beat her to it.

"Look at it logically. Would you lure a man into a room and kill him with a knife that you knew would be traced to you?"

"It doesn't add up, Carol. Had it been some knife other than the one he stole from Riggson, I'd say you were right. But anyone stopping to think about how he was going to commit the murder would know the knife would be recognized. You're way off base."

"What's *your* theory, then?" She pouted. I didn't like it. Girls who are big enough to take care of themselves just don't look good with their lower lips sticking out like shelves. Ma interrupted that thought when she came shuffling through the kitchen door to take our order.

Carol ordered Salisbury steak and so did I before she reminded me she had asked a question.

"Go ahead. Tell me your theory," she challenged. "It can't be too different from mine."

"Well," I started, then stopped. "We'll talk about it after we eat. I don't want to spoil lunch."

I was talking too much. I had started to tell her what I thought about Petey Basquez's demise. I was certain it was murder in spite of Mark's stupid theory about him throwing himself on the knife. I was pretty sure, too, that Petey hadn't killed Hickory Taite.

I knew something about death in the desert. I had seen enough of it in the Gulf War. The condition of the body when we moved it was enough to convince me the boy had been dead before Hickory Taite had been found in my bed.

But there was a reason for not expounding on my theory. Without the apron, the knife, and the lemon he was continually denuding, the bartender from the hotel seemed a little out of place. He was staring placidly into the glass of water Ma had set before him, but he had been listening to every word we'd said.

I frowned as I looked back at Carol again. I couldn't help wondering about her, too.

Chapter Twelve

It was after 1:00 when we got back to the hotel. Sitting behind the check-in desk, Riggson was writing on a yellow legal pad when we came in, but he put down his pen immediately.

"What's Ma Hanrahan got to eat? Anything different?"

"The usual Friday menu. The same old thing plus fish," Carol told him.

"Want me to take over?"

"It'd help till I've eaten." Riggson came out from behind the desk. "I'm gettin' an old friend to come up from Calexico and help out till we get organized again." He frowned, staring at her.

"You didn't get any sleep last night, did you?" He was looking at the circles under her eyes, and I wondered why he hadn't noticed them when we'd come back from the Mud Pots. He'd had lots on his mind, I surmised.

"Not much. Just a couple of short naps."

"Tell you what. I'll go over to Ma's for chow, then I'll come back and handle things while you get some rest."

"It isn't that bad," Carol protested. "I can manage."

Riggson shook his head. "I'll be back. I want you healthy in the morning. We've got a lot of work to catch up on. This mess has thrown us way off schedule."

We sat on an overstuffed sofa after Riggson left, and I told Carol a little about what I'd done in my life. I told her some funny stories about my first hitch in the Marines. I told her how I'd come out of journalism school and gone to work for eighty bucks a week as a cub reporter in Baltimore. I threw in a couple of anecdotes about that, then jumped to the job as a police reporter I'd held down in Philadelphia, and how Johnny Ferguson and I used to get each other out of jams with the city editor. She laughed with me, and I was beginning to feel better than I had since she'd pounded on my door to wake me up.

"Where's this Johnny Ferguson now? Maybe he could help you get back on your feet." Her hand was on mine and she squeezed it. "You're never going to get ahead bumming around the country, Sam. Why not try to get some of your friends to help?"

I'd been talking too much ever since I hit the town. And most of that talk had been with Carol. That first night I'd walked her home, trying to find out things about this town, what kind of place I'd happened into. But I'd also told her things about myself before I kissed her good night. Then at lunch, I'd almost told her what I thought about the Taite murder and Petey Basquez's death. Had she been trying to pump me by telling me her theory of the murder, trying to get me to tell mine? I would have, too, had I not caught Eddie, the bartender, listening. And now it was Johnny Ferguson. Why was she asking where he was? Did she know about my phone calls to San Francisco?

Still, beyond idle curiosity, I couldn't see why she'd want to know where Johnny was. Chet Riggson could have told her if she really wanted to know. Chet had been at the jail when Gould and Jeff Street had questioned me. I'd told them I was trying to get to San Francisco where Johnny'd be able to fix me up with a job.

''Johnny's in San Francisco,'' I told her. ''But I used up all my friends during my drinking period. None of them want to take a chance on me anymore.'' Not quite true, but it answered her question.

She stood up then and pointed. Through the front door I could see Chet coming across the square. He said something to one of the Mexican kids sitting there in the shade and laughed at something the boy said.

Riggson came in and told Carol to go home. She started to argue with him, but he insisted she go to bed. I was glad the big, lumbering man had come back when he did. I needed to think.

In the bar, Eddie was back on duty. He nodded as I ordered a cup of the coffee he brewed behind the bar. I half expected him to say something about seeing me at lunch. Instead, he surprised me.

''On the house. I'll catch you on the next one.''

''Thanks.'' He had left the eating place before Carol and me, nodding at us as he got up to pay the check. That had been his only acknowledgment, but I was certain he had been listening to every word we had said.

I stared at him over the edge of my cup as he picked up his paring knife and split the skin of a lemon down one side. I might as well have been on the other side of the world for all the notice he gave me. As much time as he spent stripping lemons, he must have a whole refrigerator full of twisted strips of peel. And why the free coffee?

Suddenly a word slipped into my mind: paranoia! I was trying to read hidden thoughts into every move anyone made. I was jumpy. It was the first time I recognized the tightness of my nerves. I'd thought Carol was trying to pump me, and now I was wondering why the bartender should offer me free coffee. It was foolish. After all, women are noted for the number of questions they can ask in a given period. As for bartenders, regular customers tend to take their business elsewhere if they don't get a free drink from time to time.

I felt a little better as I finished off the coffee and set the cup down.

"I'm ready to pay the damages on another one," I said. Nerves. Three bodies in two days would make anyone jumpy, not to mention all the coffee. No one could blame me for being nerved up.

"How about that beer you offered me the other day?"

Teala Locket was standing just inside the door, when I turned on the bar stool to look at her. Her hair looked less brassy in the dim light than it had in my room the day before. Her features appeared to be totally devoid of makeup.

"Sure. Pull up a stool."

"Let's sit in a booth. Ladylike cocktail waitresses don't sit at bars," she informed me. "Not even with escorts."

I slid off the stool and followed her to the last booth at the rear of the room. She sat down so she could see the door, and I slid in opposite her. I felt a tinge of irritation.

She had my seat. I have always liked to see who's coming and going, no matter where I am.

"Beer all you want, Teala?" the bartender called. He had my coffee sitting on a tray in what I took to be a fresh cup.

"That's good enough." She looked at me and smiled. "You're getting to be a well-known character around town. People getting killed in your room, people getting killed trying to get into your room, and you're still around when the killer commits suicide."

"Oh? Where'd you get all this?"

"It's all over town, Sam. You're a local celebrity. Not every stranger can come into a town this size and get mixed up with three corpses in so short a time. In fact, I doubt it's happened since frontier days." I heard no hint of sarcasm in her voice despite the words. "Some people have to hang out for years before bodies drop around them."

The bartender brought back our drinks and moved them off the tray. I handed him a five and told him to keep the change.

"The story going around town has it that Petey committed suicide when he found out the law was on his trail," the girl said. "What do you think?"

I shook my head, and my suspicions about Carol and the bartender returned. Paranoia? I remembered something Johnny Ferguson had said long ago in Philadelphia: *"Sam, you're awfully paranoid. Problem is that you're usually right!"*

"I don't know what to think," I told her, thinking about Johnny's declaration. "I guess that's as logical a solution as any other."

She poured her glass half full of beer. The bartender knew her choice and had brought a Budweiser Light.

"I don't know. Maybe I'm wrong. I don't think Charlie Maxwell was trying to get into your room last night."

"What do you mean?"

"Maxwell was as crazy a duck as ever hit this town. I know what I'm talking about. I'll bet big odds he was looking for my room instead of yours." She meant it, and when I saw the scowl on her face, I knew what she was trying to get across.

"Maxwell was that kind of a guy?"

"I've heard some strange stories about him. He liked to go down to Mexicali, and talk came back about what he did to some of the girls. And he never missed a chance to make a dirty crack at me. I put up with a lot from him, working here and living in the hotel."

"What kind of stories have you heard?"

"You know how it is. Working in a bar, I hear men talking. Like I told you before, they consider me part of the furniture. Talk is that Charlie had a real sadistic streak, but I don't know any details." She didn't bother to lower her voice to tell me that, and when I looked up, the bartender was staring in our direction.

"You really think he was looking for you?" I asked. She was pale without her makeup that I was used to seeing her wear, and I wondered whether it was the paleness of fear. Her eyes were flat and dull, and little red slivers in the corner gave her away. She hadn't had much sleep, if any.

"I'd be a lot better off if I'd never left San Diego," Teala said. "There I didn't have old men trying to crawl in my windows."

I finished my coffee and when I asked if she wanted another beer, she shook her head.

"Beer makes me fat quicker'n anything else."

"How about San Diego? What kind of work did you do there?"

"Same thing. I made good tips when the Pacific Fleet was in. All that changed, with most of the Navy and Marines spread all over the world."

"That why you come down here?"

"I was fed up with San Diego, and I heard this was a lively town when the migrants are here for the harvest. It sounded like a good deal. I've been here over a year now."

"I'm surprised they ever let you get out of San Diego," I told her. She cocked her head to one side and stared at me curiously, wondering, I suppose, if I was kidding.

"Didn't Jeff Street talk you into coming down here? He seems to be the man in your life."

She straightened and poured the rest of the beer into the glass. "I never saw Jeff Street until I'd been here at least a month. As for him, I play the field. He knows that."

Her voice was low as she moved her beer bottle and leaned toward me. "You're awful interested in who's my chief passion. How do you know it isn't you?" Her lips were near mine and they looked thin and blue without lipstick.

"I don't know."

She leaned far over the table and kissed me then. I kissed her back. One of us knocked over her empty beer bottle. It broke on the floor before we pulled apart. When I looked up, Marks, the coroner/mortician, was standing midway down the bar, staring. He turned and winked at the bartender, trying to hide the laughter curling his lips. I looked at Teala. She was laughing, too.

Chapter Thirteen

After the scene in the bar, I'd walked up the stairs with Teala. She was still kidding me about kissing her when she went into her room. I went into my own room and sat down on the edge of the bed.

I still felt a little foolish about the situation in the bar—and the way Riggson had grinned when I'd walked through the lobby with her. Riggson and Marks were friends, and once the coroner told him what he had seen, Carol would be the next to hear it. The facts wouldn't be straight when she heard the story, either. They never are in a small town. I didn't want that to happen, but you can't stop gossip.

I kicked off my shoes and tried to read a magazine, but I would read a paragraph or so only to have the print seem to blur and slide away from my eyes. Then my mind would be skipping back over the happenings of the past two days. That was when I decided on the pool hall. I didn't know where it was, but it stood to reason a town the size of Beale should have at least one. Pool halls are institutions sacred to men.

That was where I spent the afternoon and managed to

run three dollars of Riggson's money into eleven before a little Mexican boy came looking for me. I almost missed the bank shot I was executing, when he pulled at my shirt sleeve.

"Señor Riggson wants you at the hotel."

"Okay, I'll be right along," I told him. I cleared the other four balls off the table while the man I was playing grumbled about my luck.

The sun had died and the streetlights were on. My nerves had loosened up during the afternoon in the pool hall and the affairs of the past two days had been crowded into the back of my mind. Following the dark figure of the Mexican boy through the park, I found myself flexing my fingers nervously. The palm trees cast dark shadows across our path, and I caught myself staring at the dark trunks, expecting to see things I knew weren't there.

"How about workin' tonight, Light?" Riggson asked when I came into the lobby. He was sitting in the overstuffed sofa with his booted feet spread in front of him, pipe clenched tightly between his teeth. It bobbled slightly as he spoke. "I need someone to handle the desk while I catch up on some sleep."

"Sure. Anything to it except having people make out registration cards, then handing them their keys?" I owed him the fifty dollars he had advanced the day he had hired me. There wasn't much I could do to talk my way out of the job.

"There's a little more to it than that. The object is to see they pay before they leave. The best way is to make sure there's a credit card. If not, it's cash up front." He stood up. "Here, I'll show you what rooms're vacant."

I followed him behind the desk. He pointed to the keyboard and ran his finger along the row of numbers pasted beneath the keys, pointing out the numbers of the rooms that were unoccupied. Beside the keyboard was a list of the permanent tenants and their assigned room numbers.

"Be real sure not to rent any of the regular tenant rooms," he instructed. "Teala wouldn't care for it a bit, if you let some stranger into her room to spend the night." He offered me a knowing grin.

I felt the warm blood tingling behind my ears, and I hoped my sunburn was covering the blush I felt. Riggson had seen me walk upstairs with Teala, and he probably had heard about the kiss from Marks or Eddie.

"I'm going upstairs to crawl in bed and read myself to sleep," he said. "Don't wake me up, even if this place is on fire."

I said good night to him as he dragged himself up the stairway. I sat down in the swivel chair there behind the desk and tried to straighten out some of the things that had started to crowd back into my mind as soon as my pool game was interrupted.

I picked up a pad of paper and started to sketch a floor plan of the building. I drew in the lobby and the barroom, then got up to look around. I found two doors under the stairway. The first opened into a storeroom that was filled with dusty, broken furniture. The other door was to the room that had been occupied by Maxwell. It stood to reason a live-in desk clerk would live on the first floor.

The room had been stripped. All of the dead man's personal effects were gone, and the room had not been made up. The blankets had been torn off the bed and tossed on a chair, and the drawers of the bureau were standing open. Street and Gould hadn't missed a trick.

I went back to the desk and drew the two rooms into my floor plan and tore the page off of the pad, laying it aside.

The second floor was harder. The first thing I sketched in was the long hallway and the two stairways, the one coming down to the lobby and the other leading down to the alley in the rear of the building. I used the keyboard and the list of permanent residents as references in marking out the squares representing the rooms on that floor. Then, in the proper square, I wrote the name of the occupant and the room number. Myself, Riggson, Teala Locket, Jeff Street, one of the town barbers, and five men working on Riggson's irrigation project had rooms up there.

I sat there for a few minutes, chewing the eraser on my pencil, staring at my sketch of the second floor. The room on the rear corner of the floor was the one Maxwell had given me that first day, the same room in which Hickory Taite's body had been found. It was not listed as vacant on my list, and the key was not on the board. Gould or Jeff Street would be carrying that.

The room next to that was empty, followed by my current abode and the room rented by Teala Locket. The two rooms occupied by Riggson were on the corner of the building.

On the other side of the hall was the room occupied by Jeff Street, two were vacant, then the one rented by the barber. Another empty room followed, then came the three occupied by more of Riggson's irrigation workers.

Maxwell had lived on the ground floor. That meant he must have used a window in one of the rooms to gain access to the portico running around the second story. That he might have used one of the windows at the end of the hall was less than likely. He'd have recognized the risk of being seen by someone coming out of a room or up the stairway. He had to come out of one of the rooms.

I dropped the pencil and sketch as I stood up, running my finger over the keyboard. There was no passkey, not even a hook on the keyboard for one. I searched the drawers behind the desk, too, but still no key.

When I went up the stairway, I was resorting to simple elimination in checking the doors of the rooms. All of the keys were on the board except the one to the room where Taite's body had been found and Riggson's key, which he had taken up with him. That meant Chet Riggson was the only man in at the moment.

The hall was lighted by one dim lamp hanging from the ceiling right at the top of the stairs, and it cast long, strange shadows before me as I went down the hall to the rear end of the building. I tried the knobs on both sides of the hall, skipping the one to which the sheriff was holding the key. I skipped my own door and Riggson's, too.

All the way along I moved quietly, keeping as close to the wall as possible. I didn't want flickering shadows bringing the hotel owner out of his room to find my snooping.

As I went back down the stairs, I accepted the fact that my investigation had been a waste of time. The only doors that had been locked had been my own, which I hadn't bothered to check, and Teala Locket's. Riggson's might have been, too, I remembered. I hadn't checked it either, for fear of waking him.

The hotel's customers had either trusting natures or they had nothing worth stealing. All the other doors had been unlocked, and Maxwell could have used any of them to gain access to the roof.

The switchboard behind the desk brought me out of my

thoughts as I neared the bottom of the stairs. The buzzer was chattering steadily. It was Ferguson. He had heard about Basquez's death, and he was more than slightly irritated.

"What the devil are you down there for, if it's not to keep me posted?" he demanded.

"Wait a minute, Johnny. You better have the operator switch this call to the pay phone."

By the time the call was switched and I had crowded into the booth and pulled the door shut, he had cooled off a little bit. He was willing to listen.

"How'd you find out about Basquez?" I asked him.

"There was an all-points bulletin out on him." His tone was a mixture of disgust and sarcasm. "The report of his demise came with your sheriff's cancellation of the APB. The kid who covers our police department found out that much."

"Well, there's no doubt about his being dead. The coroner hasn't ordered an inquest yet, but he will. The kid died under what might be termed mysterious circumstances."

"Murdered?"

"I don't know. The guy who doubles as county coroner seems to think it was suicide. He may be looking for the easy way out, but he knows more about those things than I do. I'll try to keep you posted on what happens, but it's hard."

"I understand, Sam." His words were sympathetic, but his tone was not. He was still miffed. "I don't know how much longer we're going to be able to carry on this masquerade of yours. They're sure to find out pretty soon that you're working for us. Any other reporter hit there yet?"

"I haven't seen anyone that has that look."

"I thought not. We're the only paper in town that's carried anything on the Taite murder or the Maxwell killing. Other papers were completely out in the rain on both of them. Actually, they probably don't even care at this point, but they will."

I wondered if I should tell him my theory that Petey Basquez had been killed before the old prospector. I decided against it.

"Those prints you sent up here—"

"What about them?" I demanded.

"Got good service on them. They got here in this afternoon's mail and I put a friend of mine to work on them. Good scoop story when we want to spring it. I'll sit on it for a while."

"What've you got?" I was impatient.

"Don't get in a hurry. Maybe you know now how I felt when you didn't phone in the Basquez story." He paused to see if I was going to react, then went on.

"Taite's real name was Andrew Harlan, and he did time in San Quentin back in the Sixties. Got mixed up in a property swindle of some kind and got four years out of it."

I wished I had a pencil and notebook for what he was telling me. I tried to line the facts up in an orderly manner in my mind as I listened.

"Harlan dropped out of sight totally for about ten years after he got out of the pen. As far as we've learned, no one saw or heard from him in that time," Johnny's voice said over the wire. "Then he popped up in Los Angeles and started investing in property. He's been buying land from time to time ever since. They also claim he owns more than half a million in real estate right here in San Francisco.''

''Where'd he get tangled up in this property swindle?''

''That was in L.A., too.'' Johnny answered. ''But when he popped up here and started buying properties, the locals checked on him. They were afraid he was building up something for the suckers, again. This time, though, all his negotiations were strictly legal. He has a house in L.A., but neighbors say it's closed up most of the time. A guy across the street said he hadn't seen Harlan in more than six months.''

''Anything else?''

''Just that he has a half-brother we haven't been able to locate yet. I'll let you know if we find out anything on him.''

''You might try to find out where a penniless prospector was getting the money to buy all these properties,'' I offered.

''You're closer to the body than we are,'' came the answer. ''*You* find out!''

He hung up before I remembered that I hadn't told him about someone stealing the other copies of Hickory Taite's fingerprints and the pistol that killed Maxwell. I started to call him back, then decided I'd hold that info until the next time he groused about my not doing my job.

Chapter Fourteen

Any ideas I might have entertained about Riggson putting me to work on the desk and forgetting about me died the next morning when the bus from Calexico pulled in.

At 8:00 Riggson relieved me, so I sauntered over to Ma's for breakfast. When I came back to the hotel, he left, saying he would be at his office.

I settled down on the sofa and was watching the street when I saw the bus go past. The regular bus stop was across the square at the other hotel. It was closer to the highway and easier for the bus to reach over the town's narrow streets.

I felt better than I had since I had gotten into town. I'd slept in the bed that had belonged to Maxwell, using the blankets I found piled on the one chair. That was the first good night's sleep I'd had since leaving Miami, and I'd gone through the night without a single dream that I could recall. The heat had brought me out of it at 7:00. The room wasn't air-conditioned like the rest of the hotel, and I woke up covered with an oily coating of perspiration.

I stood up from the sofa as the woman carrying the suitcase came through the door. She stood looking around the lobby for a moment.

"Where can I find Chester Riggson?" she asked. Her voice was pitched so low I had trouble understanding her.

"He said he was going to his office, ma'am. Can I help you?"

"I don't really think so. Chester wanted to see me as soon as I got in." She seemed to sigh through the whole sentence, as though she had been through this sort of thing before and was resigned to not finding Riggson waiting for her.

"I'll get him on the phone for you," I told her, picking up her bag and moving it to the front of the desk.

I dialed Riggson's number and Carol answered. When she heard my voice, she suddenly became totally formal. It was apparent someone had told her about Teala Locket kissing me in the bar. I wondered whether Riggson had been the one to tell her. He came on the line.

"Riggson here."

"This is Sam. A lady here wants to talk with you."

"Who is it? Helen Berber?"

"Didn't say. Tall, nearing forty, blondish hair, and nice skin?" I was watching her as she stood in the center of the lobby floor. The description fit and I told him so.

"That's Helen. Put her on."

She was smiling at me as she took the phone. I smiled back and went into the room where I had slept to make the bed. I didn't know whether the hired help rated room service, and it was something to do while I was waiting. There came a knock on the door as I tucked in the sheets. Helen Berber was standing there.

"Chester says he wants me to take over the desk for a few days."

"I'm ready to abdicate right now."

"No." She shook her head. "You're to stay here this morning and show me what it's all about. Chester said you didn't have anything else to do." She stared at me, head cocked to one side in question. "You don't, do you?"

I pointed to her bags. "Did he say where he wanted you bunked?"

"He said for you to put me in one of the empty rooms."

I put her in the vacant room next to Riggson's layout, making certain there were clean towels in the bathroom and clean sheets on the bed. I hadn't seen the housekeeper all morning and wondered whether she was coming in. As I started back down the stairway, Helen Berber was right behind me.

"I can unpack this evening," she explained. "Right now I'd better stay with you, until I find out what it is Chester expects me to do."

The way she called Riggson by his first name reminded me of an old maid aunt who had lived with us when I was a kid. Everyone in the family had called me Sam except her. She always called me Samuel, and I never had the heart to tell her I didn't like it. This was different, though. Helen Berber didn't look like my aunt. Even with middle age creeping up, her figure was trim enough to pass for twenty-five, and there wasn't a line in her face. It was an oval face with a thin, well-shaped nose and deep-blue eyes under blond lashes.

Her lips were drawn in a little Cupid's bow, and I noticed she had neglected to cover part of her lower lip with lipstick. That would have ruined the shape of the bow. At first

I had thought the color in her cheeks was natural, but now, looking at her closely, I could see she had taken great care in putting on her makeup. She didn't look at all like my aunt, and as I glanced at her I knew that I wasn't going to feel the same toward her as I had my aunt.

"You haven't been here long, have you?" she asked, staring at me with a show of curiosity. "I don't remember seeing you before."

"No, ma'am. I'm just passing through. Working for Riggson till he gets himself squared around again, same as you are."

"Poor Chester. He needs someone to look after him with Bertha gone. He just can't seem to get along without a woman." It was strange, the little sigh she gave with that announcement. People may age rapidly and all that in a desert climate, I know, but they don't usually adopt her maternal attitude. Besides, Chet Riggson had to be at least ten years older than her. It was even more strange that she would speak of him as she would a little boy. She caught me looking at her and smiled.

"I've known Chester for a long time. I went to school with his wife, and I was a bridesmaid at their wedding."

"What happened to his wife?" I asked. Riggson had said something about inheriting land from her.

"She died in a fire about eight years ago. Nearly nine now. And Chester took it hard for a long time. He'd have sold everything and left town if we hadn't talked him into staying."

"Her house burned, or what?"

She nodded. "That's right. Burned clear to the ground before the fire trucks even got there. In this climate, wood dries into tinder overnight. It was horrible."

''Must have been pretty tough on him.'' I nodded agreement with her thinking.

''He'd have gone back to being as bad as he was when he first came to town if some of us hadn't made him listen to reason. He'd have ended up just another drunken tramp.''

''Riggson?'' I was all attention. ''A tramp?''

She shook her head at me. ''No, he wasn't that bad. He had a little money when he came to town, I guess. As long as you have money, you can't be classed as a tramp, can you?''

She was looking at me and I wondered how much Riggson had told her about my own arrival in town. I shook my head, trying to suppress a scowl. ''Never given it much thought, but I never figured Riggson for a one-time drifter.''

I was trying to pump her and be subtle at the same time. It was obvious she liked to gossip, but I'd have to be careful.

''Chet came through here on his way to Salinas or someplace up north, but he stayed over for a few days and went to work for Bertha's father. That was Rod Street. He was one of the pioneers in bringing water into this valley, and he had his problems.

''One big problem was in keeping a foreman who was tough enough to handle some of the hardcases that made up the crew. It took Chester a little time to get into the swing of things, but when he did, Rod made him his foreman and put him on a good salary. By then, Chet had forgotten all about why he'd wanted to go to Salinas to harvest peaches or whatever it was.''

We were seated on the lobby sofa, when she suddenly stood up, looking down at me with a touch of impatience.

"You have to show me what goes on here. Chester's coming back here at noon, and I want to surprise him with how much I know about the hotel business."

I led the way behind the desk and pointed to the board holding the keys.

"There isn't much to it. These are the keys to the rooms and these are numbers of the empty ones." I was pointing to the slip of paper on which I had jotted the numbers the night before. "If someone comes in to rent a room, assign him one of these. Better scratch off the room we just moved you into. You don't want to rent that one again."

She stopped me abruptly. "I forgot! Chester said to tell you the maid won't be in today. Her brother died yesterday."

I was staring at her. "Did Riggson mention the brother's name by any chance?"

She offered a ladylike shrug. "I think he did, but I wasn't paying much attention. Pete or Peter. Something like that."

The girl I'd found in my room, fumbling with my Colt .45, was the maid Helen was talking about. I wondered why Riggson hadn't told me she was Petey Basquez's sister.

"That gives us another job then," I told her.

"What's that?"

"Make up all the beds in the joint."

She laughed and shook her head once more. "Don't worry about that. I'll take care of it while you watch the desk."

"I don't know where they keep the linen cart. One of

those rooms upstairs is probably a linen closet." Then I was struck by a new thought.

"If you knew Riggson's wife, you must know Jeff Street. He's her brother, isn't he? You'll probably want to see him."

She didn't answer right away, and I was certain she had guessed what I was up to. She wasn't frowning at me, though. It was something else.

"I don't know Jeff well. He was so much younger than we were. He went with an oil company in some Arab country. He was there, then in Mexico so long I never really got to know him."

"Mexico?"

"He was down there for years with some oil company. He came back for Bertha's funeral, but that was the only time in six or seven years he was here until he came back for keeps."

I had laid out a couple of registration cards for instructional purposes, but I didn't rush into my teaching mode. Shutting off such a fountain of fresh information would have been near criminal.

"That's how he got to be deputy sheriff," Helen went on, staring thoughtfully out toward the street. "Barney Gould had a young deputy who up and enlisted in the Navy. Chester probably had something to do with it, but Barney got Jeff the county job and the badge."

She turned to look at me, with a scowl. In that instant she did remind me of my own aunt. "I can't imagine it. Not enough water down here to float a toy boat, and that young man left a good job to join the Navy."

"What about the Salton Sea? It floats boats, doesn't it?"

"Oh, that!" There was a touch of disdain in her glance.

"The only people who boat out there are the fools that bought what they called beachfront estates on the other side."

I was recalling the night Chet Riggson had gotten me out of jail. I'd known then he was a power in the town, probably throughout the county. Not just anyone can come back to town after a long absence and immediately pin on a deputy sheriff's badge. There had to have been some power exerted in that accomplishment.

"Oh, look! He was on the bus with me!" Helen's outburst interrupted my evaluation of the local political scene. She was pointing toward the door. Turning, I looked him over through the glass of the door. Wearing a wrinkled Palm Beach suit, he was on the veranda, a suitcase on each side of him. He was looking over the town, then turned to pick up his bags and shoulder his way through the door and into the lobby.

He must have been on the bus when Helen had gotten on in Calexico. The expensive suit obviously had been slept in. He had a sailor straw tipped on the back of his head to reveal a streak of white forehead that had not been touched by the sun. The rest of his face down to his collar was a deep shade of pink. It was going to be interesting to see what his face looked like when it started to peel.

"This's the hotel, isn't it?" he wanted to know, but he had set his bags down and had reached for the pen and one of the registration cards I had laid out on the desk. He started to write.

"You were on the bus with me," Helen told him. "The place where we got off the bus is a hotel, too."

He nodded, not looking up from his penmanship chores.

"I tried to check in there, but they say they're full. Told me to come over here."

He pushed the filled-out card toward me, along with a credit card. I glanced at the registration card. His name was John Lawrence, and he had a San Diego address.

Helen Berger escorted the man up the stairs to show him his room, and I wandered into the bar. I was still questioning why no one had told me the hotel housekeeper was Petey Basquez's sister. That oversight—if that's what it was—was rubbing on a raw nerve. And some of the things Helen had told me about the Riggson-Street alliance had me stumped, especially the bit about Riggson drifting into town as a pea-picker. Holding the town's politics in his hand the way he seemed to made it difficult to believe he had ever been down on his luck to the point that he had to pick the fields to eat.

"What're you havin', Sam?" the bartender, Eddie, wanted to know.

"Just coffee," I told him.

"Smart. We got plenty of 'em that come in and gulp down the hard stuff, gin and tonic mostly, tryin' to keep cool. Then they step out into that heat and their knees melt. Can't tell 'em, though." He turned to full a mug from the pot on his backbar.

"Answer a question for me, Eddie. What's your last name?"

"Sebastian. Eddie Sebastian." He glanced toward the lobby entrance, as he slid the cup in front of me. "Who's runnin' the desk now?"

"Friend of Chet's. She came up from Calexico to help out till he can get things back on track."

"No one in town wanted the job, huh?" He picked up a lemon and started to cut long gashes in the yellow rind.

"I don't know. Maybe he didn't look around here for someone."

"Maybe," he agreed, concentrating on his knife work. "Either that or folks figger the place is jinxed. Three killin's in three days. And everyone messed up in 'em has some connection with this hotel."

If I had any thoughts on that particular theory, they were interrupted.

"Mind if I join you?" John Lawrence from San Diego was standing in the doorway, looking around. It was sort of like the hero in the old cowboy movies looking over the crowd before venturing into the saloon. Here, Eddie and I were the crowd.

With his hat off, Lawrence was completely bald, and the top part of his head was in total contrast to the bottom half, creating a weird Easter-egg effect. But I wasn't concentrating on his facial color scheme. I was trying to figure out two things. First, where I had known this man named Lawrence. The eyes and their expression were the giveaway. Second, I wondered what he might have looked like back in the days when he still had hair on his head.

Chapter Fifteen

I called Carol just before noon and asked her to lunch, but she put me off, saying she was going to grab a sandwich and eat at her desk. I argued, insisting I wouldn't keep her away from her work for long. She settled finally by agreeing to an early dinner when she got off work at five.

"Meet me at the hotel," I suggested. "We'll take it from there."

"Not in the bar. I can't walk in there every time I meet someone. People in this town talk."

"You don't want an after-work cocktail? Some wine?"

"Single girls don't wander in and out of bars unescorted without tongues beginning to click. You'll have to come for me."

I surrendered. "I'll see you at five."

The bald salesman from San Diego was in the lobby talking to Helen when I came out of the pay booth.

I wasn't especially hungry even though I'd asked Carol to lunch. I'd have stuffed myself just for the chance to be with her, though.

125

It had been an easy morning. I had explained the registration process to Helen and offered again to help her make up the beds in the occupied rooms, but she'd refused the offer. I had watched the desk while she took care of it.

Shoving through the front door into the heat, I paused to glance up and down the street. A yellow dog was stretched out full length in the sun at the lower corner of the square, chewing peacefully at something he held between his front paws. Cars were parked about the square, and the usual number of Mexican kids played in the shade of the park, but there was nothing else. The town was as quiet as the day I had arrived. The entire population seemed to have adopted Sheriff Gould's complacency concerning the three killings that had taken place in less than seventy-two hours.

As I walked across the square toward the jail, one of the youngsters yelled something at me in Spanish and stuck out his tongue. I was still grinning when I pushed through the sheriff's front door.

Gould was at his desk, hat in his lap, scowling at the ceiling. He looked at me, then back at the ceiling, expression unchanging.

"What're you after, Light?" His tone was a growl.

"Nothing, Sheriff. I just dropped over to chat. It's my lunch hour."

"No more work than you've done since you hit town, you could eat around the clock without affectin' Riggson's schedule."

"What's bugging you, Sheriff? I didn't think anything ever bothered you."

"Lots of things bother me."

"Like not checking on those fingerprints someone ran off with?"

"I didn't have time," he protested, straightening in his chair and putting his hat on the desk. "What's botherin' me most is you!"

"Me?" The remark about the fingerprints had gotten under his skin. With an election coming up in November, it wouldn't do for too many people to get the idea that their county's top lawman was an inefficient oaf.

"I checked your story about workin' in Miami."

"It checked out, didn't it?"

He turned his head to glare at me. "Did you know this Anthony Scarpello you worked for did time on a drug rap?"

"No." I had seen Scarpello only once, and he seemed to me to be a mild-mannered Italian-restaurant owner. You could almost smell the home-cooking when you looked at him. A little man with an easy strut and a big black mustache. Apparently I'd misjudged him.

The sheriff stood up then and walked around the desk to face me.

"Light, how're you mixed up in this stinkin' mess?" He pointed his finger at me and I could almost see the word ACCUSED stamped on the end of it.

I tried to object, but he roared, "Just that you worked for Scarpello is enough to lock you up on suspicion. And the way you've been mixed up in this thing from the beginnin' would impress any jury. Men go to the gas chamber on less!"

I said nothing, because there was nothing to say. He shuffled back to his chair and dropped into it. As he sat there in silence, staring at the wall, I noted the lines of weariness crawling back into his face. The thing was getting him down in spite of what had seemed calmness until now. His outburst was an offshoot of his frustrations.

"Find out anything on Taite?" I asked him.

He didn't even look up as he shook has head. "I'm tryin' to get a court order to dig him up an' print him again."

I couldn't tell him what I knew about Taite without implicating myself. The mood he was in, telling him would put me in one of the cells in the rear of his office.

"How about Taite's personal effects? Find anything in them?"

"We tore his room apart at the hotel. Just one little bag of old clothes. Not even a letter to tell us where he came from or who his folks are."

"Well, I'd better get moving," I told him.

"Don't hurry back. I got troubles enough without you clutterin' up my office." The scowl was gone, and he grinned weakly as I went out.

I walked back toward the hotel, wondering what I was going to do to kill time until 5:00, when I saw what appeared to be an ancient livery stable. I had noticed it the day I was seeking out the pool hall. The old barn was grayed more from wind and weather than the original paint. It was on a side street but was visible from the square.

As I drew closer, I saw that boarding horses had to be a minor facet of the operation. Inside the barn were several pieces of heavy equipment, including a county road grader. There also was a complete blacksmith shop. Apparently, they did a lot more blacksmithing to repair tractors than for shoeing horse.

I wondered whether Sheriff Gould had thought to check it out. A prospector, even a phony one, ought to have a burro, and a livery stable would be the place to keep it.

The little man who ran the place had a dirty, blue chambrey shirt and a beer breath. He was sitting in a little glass-enclosed office just inside the big sliding doors of the barn.

"What can I do for you, pardner?" He was perspiring through the shirt, and little globules of sweat coated his face, spreading upward to the top of his bald head.

"Heard you had a burro you might want to sell. Taite's animal?" I was guessing, but he nodded, jerking a thumb toward the rear of the barn.

"Animal back there that belonged to Taite all right, but I can't sell him. Sheriff Gould's tryin' to find next of kin."

"That burro's going to run up quite a bill, if they don't find Taite's folks pretty soon," I suggested. I didn't know how much a burro ate. I was winging it.

"Sheriff said if he can't find nobody, he'll see the animal's sold and I get my money."

"How about my looking him over? If I like him maybe we can make a deal and save the sheriff a lot of legal red tape."

He shook his head. "Couldn't sell him without the sheriff's say so. Tell you what, though." He wiped his forehead on the sleeve of his already wet shirt. "If Barney Gould can't find no heirs or whatever, I'll give you first bid."

"I don't want to commit myself without looking the animal over."

"He's back here in the last stall." He started to lead the way, but I stopped him.

"I can take a look. Don't want to keep you away from you work." I was being a nice guy and he liked it.

"I was just goin' out for a sandwich and a beer. Look him over and I'll be back in fifteen, maybe twenty minutes."

I edged past the machinery awaiting repair and into the stable area. There were eight or ten stalls, half of them on each side of the alleyway running back from the rear door. Each stall had a swinging gate that made it possible for the owner to turn his horse loose in the enclosure. The hayloft above had a wooden floor that served as a ceiling for the lower section of the barn. There were three horses in their stalls, all watching me with bland, disinterested eyes. I suspected they belonged to some of the local high school girls who were horse lovers.

The burro was in the last stall, lying in a mound of clean straw. Alerted, he scrambled up and stood staring at me, ears drooping forlornly, the look in his dark eyes adding to his sorrowful expression. I glanced toward the open front of the barn. The street beyond was empty.

The pack saddle hung on a large iron hook bolted to one of the heavy beams that held the building's wall. On another hook were a pack, a bundle of clothing, and a blanket roll. I took them down and laid them on the packed dirt floor of the alleyway.

There was nothing in the pack but a black coffeepot, a cast-iron frying pan, a bag of dried beans, and a little sack of pipe tobacco. I unrolled the bundle of clothing, which proved to be nothing but a mass of patched rags that had obviously been pieced together by an amateur with a needle. The blanket roll was no better. Nothing was hidden in it but another blanket. I did up the bundle of clothing and hung it on its hook. I did the same with the pack and the blanket roll, before I turned to the stall where the burro stood, watching me.

"What's the matter with you?" I asked. I stuck my hand through the boards of the gate and tickled his nose. He snorted and backed away. Then he stepped forward again, sticking his dark nose out toward my hand.

It was hard to believe an animal so dejected looking could move so swiftly. I dodged to the rear as the burro whirled and lashed out with both hind feet, splintering one of the planks in the gate. I crashed into the pack saddle hanging on the opposite wall, and went down when I tripped over something on the floor.

I swore at the burro as I got up and brushed away the straw and dirt from khakis. The pack saddle was a heavy tent-shaped rack built of what appeared to be oak, the individual pieces joined with glued dowels. The two dowels holding the frame together on one side apparently had broken when I had fallen on the saddle.

Staring down at it, I saw a pair of thin plastic tubes protruding from the hollowed-out end of the oak two-by-four. I stooped and drew one of the tubes from its hiding place. The tube, almost two feet long, was filled with small rectangles of what appeared to be a thin ceramic-like material. The tube was sealed at each end with heavy lead stoppers.

Dropping back to my knees, I turned the tube slowly in my hands, noting that the bits of material, a light gray color, caught the subdued light. A lot of things were becoming clearer, and I silently thanked the ill-tempered burro, which stood behind the gate, eyeing me with sleepy disinterest.

I started to turn, as I heard the rustle of straw behind me, but I was too late. Part of my brain exploded, blowing out the walls of my skull.

Chapter Sixteen

I smelled the compound of stale beer and cheap chewing tobacco on the man's breath even before I opened my eyes. Something wet was oozing down the back of my neck, and as I lay there, eyes closed, I wondered whether it was blood or just plain sweat. My head ached, and with every beat of my heart, the walls of my skull seemed to expand, then fall back into position. Facedown on the loose straw, I didn't want to move even when the man spoke to me.

"Come out of it, feller. You're gonna be okay." He wasn't telling me. He was pleading. "Shoulda told you 'bout that burro's kickin' habit."

I opened my eyes and turned my head slowly to look up at him.

"How you feelin'?" he asked, frowning with concern. "Jus' lay still and I'll send someone after the doc."

I felt like groaning as I pushed myself up to a sitting position, but I didn't. He was still protesting, telling me he should call a doctor, when I got up on my feet and looked at the burro. The animal was unconcernedly munching a mouthful of hay.

"I want you to see the doc. If you got a busted skull or somethin', I'll be to blame," the man argued. "How're you feelin'? Tell me somethin'!"

I shook my head and it felt like it was going to fall off. "I won't sue you. I probably won't live that long." I forced a grin and he must have felt a little better. He grinned, too.

"I shouldn't have sent you back here by yourself. He's kicked at me a coupla times, but workin' around here, I'm always lookin' out for it. I never thought to warn you."

I rubbed my hand across the wet streak on the back of my neck and looked at it. The hand was wet with perspiration. I felt the lump on my head and looked at my hand again. I felt a little better knowing it wasn't blood. Whoever had clubbed me hadn't even broken the skin. All I had was a big knot and a matching headache. The pack saddle was gone. So were the plastic tubes that had been hidden in the framework.

"You're sure you're okay? You don't feel like anything's broken?" the man asked, his frown returning as he watched me take my own physical inventory. Either he knew nothing about the saddle and the tubes full of white crystals or he was playing it smart.

"I'm okay, but I don't think I want the burro. I better get back to the hotel and lie down."

He was quick to agree. "I told you, I can't sell the critter till the sheriff says so. You're lucky you didn't get more'n just a bump on the head. A desert donkey can kick a man's head near loose from his body if it's a mind to." He followed me onto the street, patting me on the shoulder, still offering apologies.

I couldn't sleep and I still had the headache at 5:00 when I met Carol. I was on my way to Riggson's office as she had wanted, but I met her in front of one of the feed stores. The first thing I noticed was that the circles were gone from under her eyes.

"You look better," I told her. "I was just on my way to meet you."

"I got done early, and Chet left, so I closed up and started for the hotel. Thought maybe I'd catch you and your new flame smooching behind the desk or something."

"Who?" Chet Riggson had told her about Teala kissing me in the bar! That was the first thing I thought. Her answer was a total surprise.

"Helen Berber."

"Oh. Her."

"Did you think I was talking about Teala Locket? I heard about that, too."

I'd been set up. She probably had spent most of the afternoon framing it. Accuse me of something, clear me, then when I think I have my feet on solid ground, push me back into the quicksands of circumstance. People seemed to have been doing that since I had first hit the town. No reason she shouldn't have her fun.

"Teala? What'd they tell you?" I demanded with a scowl.

"Oh, someone told me about you kissing her the other afternoon."

"Me kissing her?" I exploded. "She kissed me!"

"Was it better than kissing me?"

We were in front of the hotel, and she was smug with my discomfort.

"She, at least, knows what the word passion means." My comment, meant in what I suppose was cruel jest, created a long silence.

"Riggson wants me to work late tomorrow night." She was trying to make conversation after my remark. "I'll be able to make some healthy credit card payments this month."

"And get those dark circles under your eyes again," I told her. "Why don't you knock off and go to a Spanish-language movie with me tomorrow night?"

"What's wrong with tonight? Then I could still work tomorrow night."

I shook my head.

"This is my night for getting my health back," I told her. "I got kicked in the head by a burro."

"What?" She didn't believe me.

"I was fooling around over at the livery barn and a burro knocked me out cold. Took the guy that runs the stable to bring me to." I took her hand and directed it to the lump on the back of my head.

"Maybe you'd better go to bed," she decided. "You can't run around in the night air with a concussion in the offing."

"Tomorrow night?"

She shook her head, frowning. "I can't, Sam. Really. I told Chet I'd work and I can't back out. Besides, he's way behind after what's happened the past week. He worked way late last night on things I can't handle."

"Chet actually sits down and pounds a keyboard? That kind of stuff?" I said.

"He works a lot of nights by himself, but it doesn't seem to reduce my work any. Things he takes care of never get to my desk, and that helps."

The bald one with the sunburn came up the sidewalk, Sheriff Gould at his side. I was still wondering where I'd seen John Lawrence before. I was certain he hadn't been bald then. And his name hadn't been Lawrence.

He returned my stare for a second, then returned his attention to Gould, when the sheriff said something. Carol's voice brought me out of my thoughts.

"What're you staring at, Sam?"

I shifted my eyes toward her. "Just trying to figure out what kind of a guy Sheriff Gould is. He hasn't done enough since I got here to give me much of a clue."

"Don't underestimate that man," she warned. "He never says much, but that doesn't mean he can't blow up in your face."

"He's already blown in mine." I told her what he had said after learning Tony Scarpello, my Miami employer, was a convicted felon.

"You're lucky he didn't lock you up again," she declared.

It was almost as though Gould had his own actions timed to her comment. He shuffled in our direction, the bald-headed one trailing him. He beamed maliciously from behind the sheriff's shoulder, and I groaned as I remembered that smile. I'd been right about the hair, too. He hadn't been bald back in those days, or he'd worn an excellent toupee. He had the police beat for the Philadelphia *Inquirer* when Johnny Ferguson and I had been on the competitive sheet.

Gould didn't yell at me. In fact, in later retrospect, I had the feeling he was disappointed and hurt.

"Sam, want you to meet this man. Says he used to know you back East somewhere." Gould paused and looked at me, then went on.

"Name's Burchard, he says. Mr. Burchard, this is Sam Light, one of our local but temporary citizens."

Burchard offered a malicious baring of his teeth that was supposed to be a smile. "Sam and I go back a long way," he acknowledged. "Don't we, Sam?"

Dell Burchard. That was his name. I hadn't liked him in Philadelphia, and I didn't like him now. His posing as a salesman wasn't anything to which I I actually could object. After all, I'd been passing myself off to everyone in town as a transient laborer. On Burchard, though, the masquerade looked different.

"Dell tells me he's sure you're the one writin' us up in the San Francisco papers, Sam. He showed me one of the stories a bit ago. It's your story, ain't it?"

"Yes." I nodded.

"Sam," he demanded, "can't you do nothin' in this town 'cept cause trouble?"

Perhaps I felt a little shame in that instant. If so, the feeling was obliterated by a desire to see how many of Burchard's teeth I could make him swallow. Instead, I simply stood there, as Gould hit his verbal stride.

Chapter Seventeen

Gould gave it to me with both barrels, hitting me with everything he had been saving up from that first day, when he popped me into his jail and Chet Riggson popped me right out again.

"There was somethin' funny about you right from the first, Light. There had to be some reason you was runnin' around with your nose in everyone's business, diggin' up dirt." His face was a shiny red right through his suntan. "I'd have saved us all a batch of trouble if I'd run you clean out of the county after Chet made me turn you loose."

I glanced at Carol without seeming to look away from the sheriff. She was staring at him in wonderment, mouth half open. Burchard stood behind Gould, grinning with the satisfaction of a man who had just finished off a twenty-dollar steak. I missed what Gould was saying then. I was weighing my chances of getting past him and spreading Burchard's grin all over the back of his skull. Gould pushed his face closer to me and cut off my view.

"Now get this, Light. Pretendin' to be a bum lookin' for

work has more angles than you know. Then there's your Scarpello connection. Stick your nose into my business just once more and I'll lock you up on suspicion!'' He wasn't trying to be menacing. He was just plain mad. ''And if that ain't enough. I'll think up some more charges. Murder, maybe!''

He stormed away, not looking back. Burchard went with him, giving me that grin over his shoulder. Carol and I stared at each other. Then she smiled at me.

''Changed your mind about taking me to that picture tonight? You look like you need to just relax and enjoy yourself.''

The film was a Mexican western with a plot that was ancient before Roy Rogers was old enough to buy his first pair of spurs—vaquero meets girl, they fight, he turns bad, she turns to the villain for comfort. That took up the first two reels. During my time in Florida, I had picked up some fractured Spanish from the Cubans with whom I'd worked.

In the next few reels, people were forever chasing one another over the same hill and through the same dale until the last reel when it turns out our hero isn't really bad at all. He's really a law-enforcement type in disguise. The whole thing ends with the usual hearts and prairie flowers backed by guitar and violin.

There was something different when we came out of the theater, and it took me a few seconds to decide what it was. The sky, normally star-studded at night, was clouded over. I looked up as did Carol. She read my thoughts.

''Don't worry, it's not going to rain. It never does.''

''It must rain down here sometime,'' I insisted.

She shook her head. ''Not at this time of year. A little

in the winter when they're getting all the big storms up on the coast.''

''I'll take your word for it. I'm just a tourist.''

The street on which she lived seemed dark without the benefit of a moon, and we walked along for a while without saying anything.

''What happened to you this afternoon, Sam? And don't give me that burro story again. I know better.'' She was staring at me there in the dark, turning her head for just a second to see where she was walking.

''I told you what happened.''

She shook her head. ''Sam, I saw that animal of Hickory's kick a dog once. With those steel shoes, there was nothing left of its skull. If that burro got you, there'd be a lot more damage than a bump on your head.''

We were in front of the house by then. We sat down on the grass, and I gave her the whole thing. I told her of asking the sheriff whether he'd been through Hickory Taite's stuff, and how I'd gone to the livery barn, telling the operator I was interested in buying the burro. I told her about knocking the pack saddle off the hook and when the frame broke, finding the tubes filled with what I took to be microchips.

She stared at me doubtfully, twirling her hair with her fingers. ''It couldn't have been. Taite didn't have brains enough to handle anything like that.''

''I didn't say he was handling them. He just had them. And it wasn't him who beat my head in, then walked off with the stuff. He's six feet down.''

She sat there for what seemed a long time, knees drawn up under her chin, staring down at the grass. I slid my hand up on her shoulder, but when she didn't move, I let it fall away. She looked up at me.

"Sam, he's mighty mad at you, but you'd better tell him what happened." She didn't have to tell me who she was talking about. I started to say something, but she shook her head. "It's the only thing to do, Sam. Whoever clubbed you to get that stuff is going to worry about how much you know. You may be next, when he starts wondering how you knew where that stuff was."

"I didn't know!" I protested. "It was an accident. And people don't get killed over a few dozen chips."

"Killing's no big thing along the border, Sam, and you're worrying someone besides Barney Gould!"

I sat there, staring down at the grass the same way she had a few moments before.

"Kiss me good night, then go talk to Barney. He's not a bad guy, and he has to hear about this." She hesitated, then added. "From you, Sam."

It was warm and muggy, the low clouds seeming to trap the humidity, but if I was uncomfortable, I didn't notice it then. Carol leaned against my chest, hand going up to cup the back of my neck. I kissed her for a long time before I let her go.

All of the shops around the square were dark, but there was a light in the sheriff's office. Walking back, I had been forced to accept the logic of Carol's advice about talking to Gould. Telling him about the incident in the barn might help me work my way back into his good graces. As it was, I was done as far as Johnny Ferguson and the *Citizen* were concerned. Gould was sure to give all the news breaks to Dell Burchard, who'd done a real job on me.

True, I had gotten mixed up in the murders, but through

no fault of my own. And I had managed to interest Ferguson, then had reported on the killings on my own initiative.

Dell Burchard had come into town, passing himself off as a traveling salesman in order to dig into my story, and the sheriff had accepted him. When he found we were both reporters, he'd thrown the book at me and done everything but pin Boy Scout medals on Burchard. What hurt was that I'd actually been hoboing when I'd hit town, while Dell had been reporting from behind his phony salesman persona. Of the two of us, I figured I'd been the more honest.

Gould was at his desk, concentrating on a stack of papers, when I entered. He glanced at me, then back to the papers. I waited for him to finish, but he didn't look up, again.

''I told you I didn't want you poking your nose around here anymore.''

''I came to tell you about something that happened this afternoon.''

He laid down the papers and leaned back in his chair. ''About you and the burro over at Cason's barn?''

News travels fast in a small town, but I hadn't realized was how fast.

''How'd you know?''

''Cason called me. Said you acted right odd after he brought you around. Wanted to get you a doctor, but you wouldn't go. That bothered him. That and the fact he'd never seen you before. Why'd you want to buy that burro?'' He was staring at me through half-closed eyes, and I began to wish I hadn't come. I wondered if he knew about the pack saddle and its contents, too. That's what I hit him with next.

"It wasn't the burro. Somebody clubbed me from behind. I found tubes of what I think were microchips hidden in Taite's pack saddle and someone got them." I said it fast to see what effect it would have. I was disappointed. He didn't even move. He simply sat there staring out of those slitted eyes as if expecting more. I didn't have anything else to tell him and I said so.

"Light, you're into somethin' that's likely to force me to lock you up. If you ain't awful careful, you're goin' to be next. I ought to lock you up in protective custody." He didn't yell at me. Instead, he explained, as a teacher might instruct a grade-school class.

"When Riggson knocked his hotel clerk off the roof with a forty-five slug, Maxwell wasn't tryin' to get into your room because he was cold."

He stood up then and came around the desk to put a hand on my shoulder as I got up. "Go get some sleep, Sam, but think over what I've said."

Back up in the mountains there was a jagged flash of lightning as I started toward the hotel. Shapeless thoughts were chasing each other around in my mind, as I wondered how far away the mountains were. Sixty or seventy miles, at least.

Why had Sheriff Gould turned so friendly? And I wondered why I hadn't heard from Johnny Ferguson. Then, for a flashing moment, I wondered what Barney Gould would do if I broke into Dell Burchard's room and and threw him out the window. I wondered about a lot of things in the short walk. I even wondered whether Carol had been serious when she'd kissed me on the lawn in front of the house.

Two giant drops of water hit me on the back of the neck, then it was over.

"How 'bout that!" I muttered to myself. It had rained after all!

Chapter Eighteen

The telephone shrilling in my ear woke me the next morning, but it took three more sharp rings for me to get my eyes open and fumble the receiver to my ear. I knew it was Johnny Ferguson before he spoke.

"Sam?"

"I'm here."

"Is it safe for me to talk over this connection?"

"Why not? Everyone in town including Dell Burchard knows I'm working for you."

He didn't say anything for a long moment. "He's there, huh? How much does he know?"

"Not as much as I do at the moment, but he's been licking the sheriff's boots till Gould thinks he's the great guru of the journalistic world."

"Where do you stand?"

"I don't," I told him bluntly. "Sheriff Gould and I aren't exactly dancing."

He took a long second of silence, then went on. "If you're reasonably sure it's safe to talk over this thing, I've got some interesting stuff for you."

146

"Shoot."

"One of my boys found a relative of Andrew Harlan's."

I was still half asleep and it took a moment for me to remember that Harlan was the name Hickory Taite had used in his property dealings in Los Angeles. He'd used the Harlan name at San Quentin, too.

"You mean Hickory Taite?"

"He has a half-brother, John Harlan. He's living in Washington, D.C., and has some sort of Civil Service job. Nothing very important."

"Has anyone notified him that his brother's dead? It might hit him a little hard to learn his brother got buried in what amounts to a pauper's grave."

"It's up to someone else to tell him, Sam. I can't. If I notified him, he'd show up in that town and tell your sheriff how he found out. If Gould's any kind of a lawman, he'd guess you snatched those fingerprints."

"Rest assured," I volunteered, "he's that kind of sheriff."

"He could have us charged with theft and suppression of evidence, misleading the law and half a dozen other things. The fact that Taite, Harlan or whatever his name was had a record wouldn't help a darn bit."

"You're right," I agreed grudgingly. Sooner or later, Barney Gould would know it all. Of that I was certain.

"You know I'm right. Ever run into a cop yet who enjoyed having a newspaper clean up his case for him?"

We used up thirty seconds or so of Pacific Bell time just thinking, then I offered another angle.

"Sheriff Gould isn't going to like it when this thing comes out whether it's now or a year from now," I told Johnny. "The longer we hold out on him the farther we're edging away from the letter of the law. We ought to tell him all we know.''

Ferguson's tone was reluctant. ''I'll call the guy in Washington. I don't guarantee I'll tell him his brother is dead, but I'll sound him out. I don't want you in more trouble.''

''With Burchard whispering in Gould's ear, I can't get in much deeper than I am,'' I told him. ''Besides, there's a new wrinkle.''

''What's that?''

''I found microchips hidden in Taite's pack saddle. He was smuggling them out of Mexico.''

There was an instant of silence, then: ''Interesting. They're trying to keep it quiet, but it seems an outfit that does top secret work in San Jose just had a couple of thousand chips stolen. They were meant for top-secret military electronics. Think about that one!''

Hanging up, I put on a clean shirt and the same trousers I'd worn the day before. All the time I was dressing and cleaning up, I kept wondering how Andrew Harlan had ever come to adopt the Taite tag.

Most criminals using an alias tend to stick close to their real names. Sometimes they keep the same first names and change the last, or possibly change both, keeping the same initials. I'd learned that as a police reporter, staring at reward circulars every day on post office walls and on police station bulletin boards. One I remembered in particular. The man had used at least a dozen different aliases, and in every case, his first name had started with E, the last name of the alias with a B. His true name had been Edwin Barton.

There seemed to be no connection at all between Andrew Harlan and Hickory Taite. The names just didn't go together, but it also was difficult to think of the late Mr. Taite as once being locked up for phony land deals. Maybe, I thought, the guy suffered a split personality, but that didn't seem likely.

The hotel lobby was empty when I passed through to the veranda. The clouds of the night before were gone, and the sun was beating down as sullenly hot as ever.

I was used to the kind of courthouses that might be classed as aborted imitations of the national Capitol, with lots of gray granite and Greek architecture. This one was different. Built of aging red brick, it was only two stories high with a wrought-iron balcony hanging out over the street. A wooden cupola that looked like a later addition topped the structure. I suspected the architecture was of the 1880s, and there was none of the gray, forbidding atmosphere I had always connected with the word court.

I went in the front door and started down the wide corridor, watching the painted signs on the ground glass doors. I passed a judge's chambers, the courtroom, and a door that said WOMEN ONLY before I found the door I wanted.

The title, County Clerk, probably had been painted on the frosted glass door several decades before. All that was left of the original legend was the faint, black outline of the words. I pushed through the door that opened on oiled hinges and approached the long counter that ran across the room. The counter, a couple of desks, several long rows of tall filing cabinets, and a vault made up the furnishings. Through the windows I could see an expanse of green grass and one lone palm tree. I wondered about the town's source of water, realizing we tend to take such things for granted.

''What can I do for you this morning, sir?'' The voice

came from behind me, and I whirled to see the little man who had apparently followed me into the office.

"Want to check some of your records," I told him. "My name's Sam Light."

"What records did you want to see, Mr. Light?" He was professionally pleasant, smiling at me behind the lenses of his glasses. Stuck away there in that office, you'd expect him to be pretty pale, but he wore a suntan that would be the envy of some of the Hollywood beach gods.

"I'd like to find out whether or not you have a land owner in the county by the name of Harlan," I told him. "Andrew Harlan."

"Name's not familiar, but I'll look. Is he a resident of the county?" He went behind the counter and lost himself behind one of the tall filing cases.

"I think he lived in Los Angeles. I'm not sure, though."

I had expected to see a bank of computers in this office, but there was none. It took him probably ten minutes to locate the proper documents, and when he did, they didn't make much sense.

Andrew Harlan was on record as owning a piece of desert land on the west side of the Salton Sea that amounted to a little over two thousand acres.

"He's owned it for around eight years," the clerk told me. "Pretty foolish move, buying land up there, where it's sixty or seventy miles from any irrigation canal."

"Would there be enough cover out there to graze cattle or sheep?" I was looking for a reason for such a buy. The clerk shook his head.

"A cow would have to cruise at about thirty miles an hour just to keep ahead of starvation," he said with a wry smile. "Too bad he didn't have sense enough to sink his money in land on this side of the Salton Sea, where he could get water to it.''

''Right,'' I agreed. ''That land must be worth a mint by now.''

''Say, it's coming back to me now. There were some back taxes due on that land a while back. A gent I'd never seen before came in and paid them.''

''An old man with a gray beard and long hair?'' I asked.

The clerk, frowning now in concentration, shook his head. ''This was a young fellow. He paid up the taxes in cash, and I've never seen him since.''

I remembered what Hickory Taite had told me about knowing where the old Spanish treasure ship was located. He had related the story only hours before he had been killed. The obvious answer was that the legendary treasure ship was on his land.

''Where is this stretch of land Andrew Harlan owns?'' I asked. I watched as the clerk turned to a map of the county that was mounted on the wall. He traced a section out with his finger that was practically on the northern line of the county. The square of land was ten miles from the Salton Sea. Unless the Sea had been a whole lot larger three hundred years ago, Hickory Taite hadn't found any treasure ship out there in that sand.

And if Hickory Taite was actually Andrew Harlan, who was the young man who had showed up to pay the taxes? And why were they paid in cash?

Chapter Nineteen

Walking back to the hotel, I pondered the fact that the clerk hadn't questioned my open curiosity about Andrew Harlan and his properties. He had been happy just for the opportunity to show off his knowledge and his files covering the county. A truly fine trait of humanity, from an investigative reporter's viewpoint!

Helen Berber spoke to me from behind the desk as I entered the hotel lobby, and I said something conventional to her as I strode into the bar. It had been a hot walk from the courthouse, and the clean shirt I had put on earlier was dark with perspiration.

I had been reasonably happy with life until I entered the bar. Sheriff Gould and Dell Burchard were perched on adjoining stools. My outlook changed as Burchard first eyed me for a moment in the long mirror behind the bar, then turned on his stool.

"Well, well! Skidrow's answer to James Michener has come to honor us with his presence. Hail the Bard of the Flophouses!" He still wore that innocent, satisfied grin, but it didn't reduce the bite of his words.

''Better that than being a glorified copy boy, skinhead!''
I knew I had struck a nerve. He colored visibly, and it
wasn't his sunburn. He stared helplessly for just a flash
before the innocent little smile took control of his lips
again.

''Shut up, both of you or I'll lock you up for disturbing
the peace,'' Gould growled. He didn't turn around, but sat
there, glaring at us both in the mirror.

The bartender was polishing glasses down at the end of
the bar. There wasn't a lemon in sight. He put down his
towel long enough to ask me what I was going to have. Or
maybe he did it to help Gould break up the word-fest between Burchard and myself. I ordered coffee and stared at
my reflection in the mirror, until he brought a steaming cup
and set it in front of me. I shoved a dollar bill at him, still
eyeing my image in the mirror.

I looked a lot better than I had when I'd first hit town.
My face was fuller and I didn't look so tired. Not having
several days' growth of beard hanging all over my face and
wearing relatively clean clothes could have something to
do with it.

That was when I caught Gould's eyes in the reflection.
He was staring at me thoughtfully through those half-closed
lids the same way he had the night before in his office. He
saw that I had caught him giving me the once over and
dropped his eyes back to his beer glass.

I glanced at Burchard and grinned to myself. He hadn't
liked being admonished by the sheriff. Maybe he didn't
have as much of an edge as I had thought. He was staring
solemnly at his empty glass as he twisted it nervously between his fingers. He was sucking his lower lip, chewing
at it diligently with his front teeth. No one was saying any-

thing. That was when Helen stuck her head through the connecting doorway to announce I was wanted on the telephone. I followed her into the lobby.

"Long distance from San Francisco." She nodded toward the phone booth in the corner. "He's calling on that. I didn't think you'd want the opposition knowing what you were doing."

"Opposition?"

"Burchard, I mean. He's a reporter, too, isn't he?"

"You know all about us, huh?"

She offered that prim nod once more. "Everybody in town must know by now."

I edged into the phone booth, pulling the folding door shut and thinking unkindly about small towns in general.

"Hello, Johnny," I said, when the operator told us to go ahead.

"Hi. I just talked to Edwin Harlan, Sam. He's coming out here as soon as he can arrange some vacation and book a seat on a plane."

"Oh? How much'd you tell him?"

"Everything. I ran him down at the Department of Interior where he works. I brought him up to date on everything we know. He knew his brother had been in San Quentin, but stuff like the treasure ship really blew him away."

"What's going to happen when he pops up here claiming to be Hickory Taite's brother, when Taite wasn't even the old guy's name? Barney Gould isn't going to like that!"

"That's one of the things we talked about, Sam," Johnny said. "I laid our cards right out on the table and told him you're mixed up in this thing deeper that any of us like. He's willing to cooperate with the paper."

"What else did he say?"

"Not an awful lot. He told me he hadn't seen his brother since before he went to San Quentin. They've corresponded from time to time since, but nothing that could be called regular."

"Did he ever send mail to Taite at a Beale address?" I asked.

"I asked him about that. He's never heard of Hickory Taite. All his letters were sent to Andrew Harlan's address in Los Angeles."

"He have anything else to offer?"

"That's about the extent of it." I knew what was coming next.

"Sam, couldn't you keep us in the loop by sending night letters instead of using long distance? Press rates are a lot cheaper, and there's less chance of an error in fact, if we get it in black and white on this end."

"There's not even a Western Union office in this town. This is the only way. Everyone knows practically every move I make as it is. As for security, even if I was able to send night letters, Burchard probably would have the info as soon as you. Maybe sooner. Whatever anyone sees, reads or even hears in this town immediately becomes public property."

"I suppose so." His tone was one of disappointment. "We'll have to put something out soon on Taite's real identity, though."

"Go ahead and break the new stuff then!" I said it casually, but I heard him gasp at the other end of the line. "Print the stuff I've given you on Hickory Taite, along with his true identity and criminal record. Might be best to save the part about finding his half-brother for another day, though. Talk to you later.'' I hung up.

I sat in the booth for perhaps two minutes, waiting to see whether he called back. When he didn't, I knew he was going to print the update.

''What're you grinning at?'' Helen demanded when I came out of the booth.

''Friend of mine just told me a story,'' I told her. ''Little too risqué for me to repeat to you.''

She sniffed at me. ''I've been around more than you may think, Sam Light. I haven't always been an old maid.''

I was still pondering that when I went back into the barroom. The only customer was Gould who was on the same stool as earlier.

''Where's your balding buddy?'' I asked. ''Trying to tap my phone call?'' In reply, the sheriff cast me a glance best described as one of total disdain.

''More coffee, Sam?'' Eddie asked.

''Not now.'' I slid onto the stool next to Gould. I was glad Dell Burchard wasn't there. I knew generally what I was going to say, but I didn't know just how to put it. Gould was unpredictable, seeming to move along easily and unconcerned, then suddenly he'd blow his stack. When he calmed down, it was as though he never had been any different. I had to put across what I wanted to tell him without getting him all worked up. That called for a cautious approach. Sort of like disarming artillery duds.

''I've come across some information maybe you'd like to know about, sheriff,'' I told him. He jerked his head up and stared at me with open doubt. ''It won't hurt to hear what I have to say.''

Gould glanced at Eddie, but he was down in the middle

of the bar doing something to the drain in the sink. I had kept my tone low enough that he couldn't hear.

"I'm listenin'. Like they say, it ain't costin' me nothing."

I shook my head. "It's a long, involved story, and a barroom's no place to tell it. Let's go up to my room."

He stared at me for an instant, then nodded, pouring the dregs of the beer into his glass. I waited while he gulped down the last swallow and wiped the back of his hand across his mouth.

"Let's go," he said.

Helen had cleaned up the room. The bed was made up and the dirty shirt I had thrown on a chair was hanging in the open closet. Gould looked around, then settled on the edge of my bed, waiting. I pulled the rickety straight-backed chair over so I would be facing him.

"How would you like to find one set of those fingerprints that were stolen?" I asked.

"Where'd you hide them?" I expected him to be angry, but he was waiting for me to make the moves. Waiting and watching.

I shook my head. "I took one set. I don't know where the others are, and I didn't take Maxwell's pistol."

Gould went on waiting, while I poured out the rest for him. I told him Taite's real name, of his prison record and his half-brother who was with the Department of Interior. I told him also about the property Taite owned.

He snorted at that. "Heck, I didn't suppose he owned nothin' more'n the clothes on his back and what he could pack on that burro." He stared at me across the foot of the bed. "This is straight stuff you're feedin' me?"

"It's all fact, Sheriff. And there's more to that burro

episode than you think. Taite's pack saddle was worth its weight many times over in gold. He was smuggling microchips in the hollowed-out saddle frame.''

''Lucky all you got was a knot on your head. You could be dead.'' His doubt and hostility were gone. ''All this may be worse than you think.''

I nodded and neither of us said anything. He rubbed his hands together, then stared at them, thinking. The two shots sounded as if they were right in my ear. The wall between my room and Teala Locket's was that thin. We both were on our feet before the third shot sounded.

Chapter Twenty

Gould was swearing hoarsely as he twisted at the knob, trying to get the door to my room open. I closed my hand over his, twisted and jerked, almost knocking him off his feet. The rush of hot air met us as we both stumbled into the hallway.

"It's Teala's room!" I yelled at the sheriff's back.

The door was half open, the body lying against it. As we pushed in, bumping against the door, she rolled heavily on the floor to lay there, staring up at us with blank, empty eyes. Gould leaned over her, as though expecting her to speak. With the small, blue hole in her throat, she was dead.

Beside the door were three suitcases and a round, flat hat box. Her clothes had cost money, I realized without really thinking about it. A two-piece suit of gray gabardine with matching suede shoes. I've never seen the outfit before, but I had seen the gun in her hand. Charlie Maxwell had carried it the night he had been shot by Riggson. It had to be the handgun stolen from Gould's desk, along with the other sets of fingerprints.

Jeff Street was hunched over Teala's body. He shook his

head and tried to speak, but no words came. All he seemed able to do was stare.

"What happened, Jeff?" Gould asked, straightening up and staring at his deputy. Street looked at him with disinterest, then returned his gaze to the body for a long moment before he said anything.

"I didn't mean to kill her, Barney, but she tried to shoot me!" His voice was low and tight. He glanced at me the same way he had at Gould a moment before.

"Better explain," the sheriff instructed, scowling.

"She told me she was going back to San Diego, but I didn't believe her. There was no reason to leave town just 'cause we had an argument!" Jeff looked at the sheriff, shaking his head slowly and without understanding. "Why'd she want to leave? Why'd she pull the gun on me?"

"I don't know, Jeff. What's the rest of it?" Gould's voice was low, too, but in a different way. My father used the same tone when I was a teenager and came to him with my first girl trouble. His voice had been understanding and kind. Gould had that same touch.

Jeff's eyes went back to the body, voice still a monotone.

"I told her I'd see her this morning, and she said not to bother. Said she was leaving and not to try to stop her. She got sore when I told her I couldn't afford to get married. I thought she'd have cooled off by now, so I came up to talk to her."

"Sit down, Jeff." Gould motioned toward the bed on the other side of the room. It had been slept in, and the sheets were crumpled in a loose bundle at its foot. "Over there."

I ripped the wrinkled cotton off the mattress, and Gould

nodded approval. The sheets covered the body, and Jeff Street squirmed onto the edge onto the bare mattress.

"What else happened?" Gould urged.

"She was ready to leave when I came up. I tried to reason with her, but she wouldn't listen." Jeff paused and looked at the floor. "When I tried to kiss her, she pulled that gun. I grabbed for it and she started pulling the trigger." He paused again and looked up at us. His face was white, and his eyes seemed sunken in his head. "One of the shots got her."

"Ever seen that gun before, Jeff?" The sheriff asked, motioning toward the sheeted body. "Remember it?"

The deputy nodded. "It was Maxwell's, wasn't it?"

Gould didn't answer. Instead, he turned to stare out the window for a moment before he turned to me.

"Light, stand over next the door. Don't let nobody in. There's a crowd down there in the street. I don't want 'em stampedin' in here soon's they get up the nerve."

I moved over to the door and closed it, trying to keep my eyes off the floor, while Gould continued staring out the window.

"Let me have your gun, Jeff. I'm afraid I have t' hold you till we get this sorted out. Just routine."

The sheriff's voice still had that note of comfort and understanding, but Jeff's head jerked erect. He started to say something, but changed his mind. He reached beneath his suit coat and removed a revolver from its holster, handing it butt first to the sheriff. He allowed his gaze to drop once more, and he seemed to be concentrating on the toes of his eelskin boots.

Gould spun the cylinder on his deputy's revolver and, satisfied with what he saw, shoved the weapon in his waistband. He came across the room and tore off a corner of the sheet I had spread over the corpse. He held the bit of fabric in one hand and reached under the sheet with it, dragging out the short-nosed revolver that had been clutched in Teala's hand. There was a crust of brown blood on the butt, but he didn't bother to wipe it off as he rolled the weapon in the cloth and stuffed it into his hip pocket.

I hadn't noticed the handbag before. Gould snaked it out from under the chair beside the body. It had been half hidden by the body and the door before I had closed it. The bag was of suede leather and matched the shoes and the gray suit the woman was wearing.

I watched as the sheriff inspected the exterior leather, then pulled the zipper open to stare inside. I stiffened involuntarily as he emptied the contents onto the seat of the chair. Amid the clutter of papers, folded letters, cosmetics, and other female paraphernalia were four long, cylindrical tubes. Each of the tubes had been cut in two to fit in her purse. One end of each carried its lead plug. The other ends were covered with pieces of silver-colored duct tape.

The sheriff glanced at me, as he picked them up, but I could tell nothing from his expression. It hadn't changed from the moment we had entered the room. He stared at the transparent tubes, turning them around and around and holding them up to the light, then turning them end for end, sliding the dull gray chips from one end to the other.

"Microchips," I told him. He nodded, not looking at me. I'd seen these tubes—or some like them—sticking out of the broken framework of a pack saddle just before someone had kicked in my skull. Suddenly the covered figure at my feet didn't seem to rate quite the degree of compassion I had been feeling. Jeff Street hadn't moved. He sat staring at his feet.

Gould was thorough. He carefully inspected each item before pushing it into a pile on the chair seat. He read each of the letters before sticking them back into their envelopes and stacked them on the pile. The four plastic containers he put back into the suede handbag. The only other thing that went into the handbag was Teala Locket's bus ticket. I caught a flashing glimpse of the stark, black lettering. It wasn't a ticket to San Diego at all. She had been bound for the border town of Calexico. Across the line was Mexicali and Mexico. And maybe someone she intended to meet.

There was a timid tap on the door then and I pulled it open a crack. Helen was in the hallway, a man on each side of her. One was the bartender. The other I'd never seen before. Behind them, on the stairway were other faces, expressions ranging from concern to a strange viciousness. The vultures had arrived!

"What happened?" Helen asked, eyes anxious. "Is everything all right?"

"The sheriff's here," I told her. "He has everything under control."

"But what's happened?" she insisted. I felt Gould at my shoulder, and I let him answer.

"There's been some trouble, Helen. Get all these people back downstairs and call for Marks."

"The place's got another corpse!" Someone on the stairway said it, and there were low rumblings as I pushed the door shut. I could hear Eddie harshly ordering the curious back to the lobby, Helen chiming in with more polite tones.

"She shouldn't have tried to run out on you, Jeff. That

was fatal. But considerin' how many people've got themselves killed, she was right to be scared.''

Gould's voice wasn't soft and fatherly anymore. It was hard and brittle in a tone that brought Jeff Street's eyes off the floor to stare at us. The shocked expression was gone, and a lot of things were suddenly clear.

''This thing's been goin' on for far too long, Jeff. I figgered out most of it some time back, but till now I couldn't prove th' things I suspected, could I?'' The sheriff paused, waiting, but Street simply stared at him, expression now hard and cold.

''You had a sweet setup, Hickory Taite usin' his burros to sneak the stuff over the border, then you usin' Charlie Maxwell and the phony one-night hotel guests to move the cheap Japanese stuff north where it got sold at U.S.-made prices. Taite brought it in and passed it to Charlie. He gave it to whatever guest was workin' with you. Then, the next day, the stuff was in L.A., Frisco, or wherever else you wanted it delivered. And you had the money in your pocket. Sweet!

''When you started killin' off your crew, so you wouldn't have to share the big one, you scared Teala. Tryin' to cut overhead that way's goin' to hang you!''

Jeff was on his feet suddenly, but Barney Gould's hand streaked to the open holster at his hip. The sixgun he leveled at his deputy was steady and deadly. I'd never seen a draw like that before, and I forgot all the thoughts I'd had about Gould's slowness and plodding attitude. That draw, like the clothes he favored, was something out of the Old West.

''You're not going nowhere, Jeff!''

''I had nothing to do with any of them!'' Street shouted.

His face wasn't white any more. It was red with rage as he stood with knees against the edge of the mattress, hands raised to shoulder level.

"When you clubbed Sam and walked off with them tubes, you didn't figger he'd come to me, did you, Jeff?" Gould was enjoying himself, spitting his words at the other man and casting him a crooked grin. "Well, he told me, and I knew enough to look around your room. There the stuff was, tucked in real neat between your shorts and T-shirts. That was foolish, thinking you was above suspicion."

Street started to speak, but Gould waved the big six-gun at him.

"Best keep your mouth shut till you see a lawyer. Anything you say'll be used at your trial."

Some of the bitterness went out of his voice then, and I caught a hint of the old weariness that had been there the first day we had met. "I'm sorry it had to come to a head this way." He waved the gun at the body beneath the sheet. "She was awful pretty to end up like this."

It was Jeff's turn to sound bitter.

"She was a greedy, double-crossing dog," he snarled.

Chapter Twenty-one

Dell Burchard was halfway down the stairway when I opened the door.

"Hey!" I knew yelling was useless, but I did it anyhow.

I hit the top of the stairway and started after him. The lobby was crowded with people, and I caught a glimpse of Helen on the sofa in the middle of the room. She looked startled as I bounded down the wooden steps behind Burchard. He was already in the phone booth, talking excitedly when I got there. He was still grinning, as he glanced out at me.

"Out of there, Burchard!" I roared at him. He waved a hand in a show of derision, and I began kicking the folding door.

Phone in one hand, he tried to hold the door shut with the other, while I jerked at the handle. It took several attempts before I was able to force it open and get my hands on him. Someone behind me was yelling. There in the narrow confines of the booth, I shook the man with all the strength I could generate, hands on his throat. I heard the glass in the half-open door break as my elbow went through it and I was dully aware of pain.

Burchard was screeching at me, hands clawing at my wrists in desperation, as I dragged him out onto the lobby floor. He kicked me and tried to pull away. I released my hold on his throat and hit him in the nose. It had been scarlet with sunburn but it turned a fish-belly shade of white as my fist forced all the blood out of the tissue. He swore at me, clawing wide-fingered at my eyes. He swung and I tasted blood after he hit me in the mouth. I went in close, fists driving. Over Burchard's shoulder I caught a swift glimpse of astonished faces and Helen's white, shocked expression.

The shocked expression on Helen's face didn't faze me. I wanted Burchard to pay for all of the fear and frustration I had suffered since coming to town. The floor shook when he fell. I stood over him for a moment, panting, fists still clenched.

''Nice touch, Light. Very nice!'' Marks offered from the circle of onlookers, a wry smile on his lips. Behind him were Eddie, the bartender, and the little man from the livery stable. My eyes went back to the coroner.

''Sheriff wants you upstairs, Marks,'' I panted. ''He's got another customer for you.''

Marks nodded. ''Anyone I know?''

''Teala Locket.'' A series of surprised gasps went around the circle. Helen Berger sat down heavily on the sofa again, and I heard her sigh, as she leaned back and shut her eyes.

The coroner was halfway up the stairs when he met Sheriff Gould. The sheriff was several steps behind the hand-cuffed Jeff Street, talking to him in low tones as he urged him downward with his drawn revolver. The gun he had taken from Jeff was still in his waistband, and he had Teala's gray suede bag under his arm. I thought again of the first time I'd seen him. He'd looked like a sheriff out of a low-budget Western film. He still looked that way, marching Jeff Street ahead of him. He cast a glance at Burchard's body there on the floor. He spoke without allowing the gun to waver from a selected area on Jeff Street's back.

"Kinda rough on him, weren't you, Sam?" It was the first friendly expression he'd ever shown me. "What're you goin' to do if he files charges?"

I shook my head. "He's probably in a hurry to leave town. They say anything's fair in love, war, and journalism!"

I glanced at Street and he returned a sullen glare. I was in the phone booth, trying to shut the broken door, when they passed me.

"Don't leave here, Sam. I need to talk to you," Gould said over his shoulder. "Go help Marks till I get back."

Burchard had saved me some trouble. The long distance operator was on the line when I picked up the dangling telephone.

"Operator, I'm calling Johnny Ferguson at the San Francisco *Citizen*. It's a collect call." I gave her the number.

The operator started to argue. "The number you gave me was for Los Angeles."

"Things have changed!" I cut in. "If Ferguson's phone's busy, cut in. This is an emergency!"

"Yes, sir!"

Johnny accepted the charges, then let me do the talking. I gave him everything. I told him of getting hit on the head and someone walking off with the microphips and I told him about the Locket killing and gave him my version of the relationship between Taite, Teala, Charlie Maxwell, and Jeff Street, all members of an organized smuggling ring. I still wasn't certain where Petey Basquez fit in to all this and told him so.

"They had a beautiful setup," I explained. "The deputy sheriff was the brains of the outfit. Posing as a harmless old desert rat, Hickory Taite was able to wander all over the border here without arousing suspicion, and he was the gang's means of getting the stuff across the line. The Border Patrol can't be everywhere at once, and Taite knew where they wouldn't be when he made his trips back across the border.

"Teala Locket and Maxwell both worked here in the hotel. It was their job to get the stuff from Taite and hand it over to the couriers who'd pay off, then take it on to L.A. It doesn't take much of that stuff to add up to a lot of money, and it looks like they were bringing it in regularly."

"What about their outlet in L.A.? Got any dope on that?" Johnny asked.

"I'll let you have it as soon as the sheriff finds out. Street'll break down sooner or later. Probably sooner," I promised. "But I think this batch of chips was going the other way. Teala had a ticket for Calexico."

There was a moment of silence "You think this may be the top secret stuff stolen up here? That the chips were bound for China, Iraq, or some other country that's trying to get in the missile business?"

"Seems logical. Street spent a lot of time in Mexico and Iraq earlier."

"Maybe I ought to tip off the FBI on this." Johnny sounded worried.

"Don't," I ordered. "Let me have Gould contact them. He's up for reelection in November. He can use the publicity."

"What've you got as proof of all this?" John wanted to know. "I need verification if we're going to run this stuff."

"No one's going to sue you for libel," I told him. "When your rewrite man works this over, have him quote a reliable source."

"Who's the reliable source?"

"Me! Print it the way I'm giving it to you!"

He didn't say anything and I went on.

"With other members of the gang getting knocked off, the girl got scared. Whatever the reason, Locket decided to pull out. She made the mistake of trying to take the top-secret stuff with her. Smuggling counterfeit chips into the States was probably small time, but it was regular. The stolen military stuff was the big time. Street killed her with the sheriff and me right in the next room. I don't think he knew we were there.

"He tried to tell us they had an argument and she was killed in the struggle over the gun she pulled. But there wasn't any argument or any struggle. I'm sure of that. The walls between those rooms are thinner than toilet paper. We'd have heard any argument."

"I'll print that much of the story, Sam, but you'd better get out and clean up some of the loose ends. How soon can you wrap it up?"

"That's what I'll be doing, when I don't have to gab with you!" I hung up without sign-off formalities. I was a little ticked that Ferguson seemed to be forgetting the hours of legwork, digging and waiting required on this sort of thing.

People were still in the lobby, standing in near-silent groups when I wrestled open the broken door of the phone booth. Burchard was nowhere in sight. Neither was Helen.

Eddie approached me as he nodded toward the stairway.

"I told your friend he'd be real smart to beat it. Eight to five says he's upstairs packing."

"Thanks, Eddie."

"I don't like him, either."

I went up the stairs three at a time and pushed into Teala Locket's room without knocking. Marks had removed the bloody sheet with which I had covered Teala's body and was on his knees, inspecting the bullet entry in the dead woman's throat. He looked up at me.

"She didn't know what hit her."

I backed into the hallway and pulled the door shut, relieved that Burchard was not at the scene with him.

I was halfway down the stairs before I noticed the blood-soaked shirt sleeve. The elbow I had stuck through the glass in the telephone booth was beginning to feel stiff, and I felt the stinging of my cut lips where Burchard had landed a blow.

The few people still in the lobby stared at me as I crossed the lobby and went out the front door. I turned and started down the sidewalk. Gould had told me not to leave the hotel, but I had to tie up a couple of those loose ends that bothered Johnny.

Chapter Twenty-two

Papers and manila file folders were stacked in neat piles on Carol's desk, but she wasn't there. The door to Riggson's private office was open, and I could see his feet propped up on the desk. I heard a few quick words, then the fumbled clicking as he hung up the telephone. As I stood watching, the feet came off the desk and he stood up where I could see him. He saw me, too.

"Come on in, Sam. Been expectin' you ever since Barney climbed your back for not tellin' him you're a reporter." He was smiling just a little as I stepped in from the outer office.

"Where's Carol?" I asked him.

"Gave her the afternoon off. She's had a rough week. Shut the door and sit down," he invited. "Just talked to Helen Berger. She told me what happened. Tough for Jeff."

"Aren't you going over?" I asked, as I pushed his office door closed, then dropped into a chair. "It is your hotel."

Riggson shook his head, his lips parted just enough one might call it a smile. "I'm keeping out of this as long as

172

I can. Jeff's Street's my brother-in-law. It could be bad for him if I went sticking my nose in before the sheriff sends for me.''

"Sit tight and wait for things to simmer down." I made it a statement of fact.

"Right." He picked a handful of clippings off his desk and held them up for me to see. "Been readin' your stuff about the situation. Pretty good, but I wish you'd made some effort to keep me and my hotel out of it."

"Two of the killings happened in your hotel, Chet. And you did kill Maxwell!"

"True," he agreed. "Reckon you have to report all of it or there wouldn't be a story."

"That's about the size of it. Where'd you get the clippings?"

"You're not the only one with friends in San Francisco. A business associate read the first story the day after Hickory Taite was killed. I asked him to send along anything else he saw. You're the only one who could've written them. Simple logic."

"Want your fifty bucks back?"

Riggson shook his head, giving me his old grin. "You earned it, workin' around the hotel for me. Want a drink?"

He didn't wait for an answer, but pulled open the top drawer of his desk and set an unopened bottle and two glasses on top. I hitched my chair closer while he ran his thumbnail around the seal on the neck of the bottle.

"This isn't as good as the last stuff," Riggson said, twisting off the cap and starting to pour whiskey into the glass nearest me. "Sorry about that.

We clinked glasses and downed the stuff before I put the question to him. I think he had been expecting it.

"How much do you know about Hickory Taite owning land up on the west side of the Salton Sea?" I asked quickly. "How'd you know his real name was Andrew Harlan?"

Riggson's smile slid off his face like snow off a roof in June. He stared at me, eyes narrowing. "What're you getting at, Light? Why the questions?"

"You probably knew Taite had a brother in the Department of Interior. As a government worker, he could pass Hickory a lot of inside info."

I put it to him straight but easy. I didn't want to excite him. I hadn't seen it, but I knew the gun was in the drawer when he'd opened it for the whiskey bottle. The drawer was still open, and when he reached for the .45, I raised my hands level with my eyes before he touched it.

"What else do you know?" His voice was flat and hoarse.

"It all goes back to Taite being Andrew Harlan and being able to use his brother," I told him. I was gambling, and I said it slowly, as if it was a hole card that I had to play carefully. I had to keep him from wondering why I'd walked into his trap so deliberately. In short, I had a problem.

"You knew the government's planning another irrigation canal that would make the other side of the Salton Sea as valuable as the property on this side. It may be nothing but rocks and sand, but with water, it'll be a gold mine. Taite's brother mentioned the irrigation plans in a letter, and Hickory had brains enough to buy up a couple of thousand acres out of drug money."

Riggson's face was the same pasty white as the day we'd gone out to the Mud Pots to bring back Petey Basquez's body. His eyes were red-rimmed and his breath was coming in the same short gasps as it had then. The big gun in his hand didn't waver. It was pointed straight at me, fingers curled tight around the black grip.

"Taite couldn't register the land without the possibility of someone recognizing him. After all, he was a well known character along the border. He paid someone to register title under his real name, then hired someone else, one of the transient workers maybe, to pay the taxes when they started to pile up."

"How much are you just guessin' at?" Chet Riggson's voice was more a growl than anything else. I felt the skin at the back of my neck begin to prickle and the hair to rise. It was the same sensation I'd experienced the night Charlie Maxwell had tried to get into my room.

In that moment, I realized I was terrified. With Jeff Street off to jail, the rest of it had looked easy, but there was nothing easy about staring down the muzzle of the well kept .45 in Riggson's big hand. I experienced a flashing replay of one of the big bullets sending Maxwell crashing through the guard rail and cartwheeling toward the ground. This same gun had killed him!

Riggson repeated his question. "How much do you really know?"

"I know most of it. I don't have to guess," I assured him.

"Go on. Tell me some more. It's interesting." His voice was still a low growl.

"Taite found out you were buying up land in the same area. It wouldn't take much for him to figure out you knew about the plans for the irrigation canal and were trying to get in on the kill. Hickory wasn't happy with what Jeff

Street was paying him, so he tried to blackmail you with what he knew.'' I paused, but Riggson knew I'd go on without any prompting.

''You wouldn't be satisfied until you owned all that land, would you, Riggson? You're the kingpin in this valley and you intend to stay on top!''

Those were dangerous words, I knew, but I had to make him talk if things were to go as I hoped.

''Hickory was counting on your dynasty complex when he tried to blackmail you. If information he had about the canal got out, you wouldn't be able to buy a single acre for all the pesos in Mexico. And you couldn't buy Taite's land, because he wouldn't sell. You had to kill him.

''The Mexican boy had stolen your knives like you said, but he returned them when you threatened to have him jailed. By killing him with one of the knives, you could make it seem like he had knocked off Taite, then committed suicide. You kill him before or after you got Taite?''

''Just keep talking. Maybe I'll learn from my mistakes.'' He shifted the pistol to his left hand as he poured himself another drink. I eyed my own empty glass, and he shook his head. ''You don't need any more.''

''My throat's awfully dry from all this talking.'' I didn't have to lie. It was true. Or maybe the dryness was a fear syndrome.

He leaned forward and poured maybe a finger into my glass, then settled back in his chair and set the bottle down.

''Easy with the hands,'' he warned. ''Keep both of them on the glass,'' he cautioned. Cupping the glass as ordered, I took a quick sip.

''I guess you figured the buzzards would take care of Petey Basquez, chewing him up so no one would ever be able to really tell what happened to him, suicide or murder. If it hadn't been for his white shirt and that silver knife handle flashing in the sun and scaring the birds, they'd have finished him off on schedule. A rough break for you.''

Riggson looked sick. I could see his nostrils flare with each breath. He was gray under his suntan. Could he have a heart condition?

''You told Taite you'd pay and to meet you in the hotel room that afternoon. That was the day he got drunk and was telling everyone he knew where the old Spanish treasure ship was. You were his treasure ship. You and his knowledge of the canal. When he showed up for the payoff, you killed him!''

I yelled that charge, and the hammer on the big six-gun flipped back under his thumb, I threw the half-full glass and catapulted out of the chair, going over the desk.

The glass missed him completely, though a little of the whiskey splashed across his face and eyes. His bullet exploded in my ear as my head hit his shoulder and spun him around.

There was another explosion as I hit the floor, I saw the gun a few feet away. I grabbed for one of Riggson's legs as he went past and got kicked in the face as the third shot exploded from the office doorway.

Riggson staggered backward and got the back door open before he fell out into the dust of the alley. Gould was standing there, looking down at him, when I rolled up to a sitting position. His gun was still ready in his hand. I got up and walked over to him.

''Right smart of me to follow you, when you didn't wait at th' hotel like I said, wasn't it, Sam?'' He shoved the revolver back in his holster as I stumbled forward to look out into the alley. Riggson was face down in the dusty gravel. As he lay there, a fly crawled inquisitively across the back of his neck and into his ear.

"What if I hadn't showed up?" the sheriff wanted to know.

I grinned at him even though it hurt. "Do you think I'm a total fool? I made sure you were following me before I closed the door to this room. I knew you'd be listening out there."

He nodded and looked around for a moment. Then he stared speculatively at the bottle on Riggson's desk. I dropped into a chair, weak and spent, reality suddenly sweeping over me.

"I don't suppose Chet'd object to us havin' one on him." He reached for the bottle. "You look like you need it."

Chapter Twenty-three

Johnny Ferguson had wired me some money with orders to be on the afternoon bus out of town. I'd argued that a couple of Federal officers were on the way from San Diego, but he said that could contact me in San Francisco, if they needed me.

There, on the veranda of the town's other hotel, my battered old suitcase was lined up with those of the other two passengers, who were waiting in the lobby's coolness. I was wearing my last clean khaki outfit and had the ticket I had bought from the desk clerk. Instead of sitting inside with the others, I was pacing up and down the sidewalk.

I had called Johnny and given him the rest of the story, including the part about Riggson. Jeff Street had admitted the microchips were stolen and were headed for some of his old friends in Iraq.

I had tried to hurry in feeding Johnny the update on the latest happenings in Beale, but I'd taken care to give it to him straight. That had taken a good deal longer than I had hoped. Then I'd called Carol, but there had been no answer.

I hadn't been able to find her any place in town, and no one had seen her.

I sat down on the steps, shaded by the overhang of the veranda roof, and looked out over the town square. Up the street, I could see the face of Riggson's hotel. One never would guess it had been the background for five deaths, all of them violent.

Over in the park, the Mexican kids were playing as they had every day since my arrival. Outwardly, the town remained unchanged in spite of all that had happened.

I had told Johnny about Riggson's plans for gaining control of the desert area on the western side of the sea, and the wrench Hickory Taite had thrown into the wheels of personal progress by trying to blackmail him.

No one would ever know for certain how it actually had happened, but I had offered Johnny my version of how Riggson had told Taite to meet him in the hotel room. Then, while the town had dozed in its midday siesta, he had come down the alley and sneaked up the rear stairway to stab Taite in what he had taken to be an empty room. Had it not been rented to me by Maxwell, it might have been at least a day before the murder was discovered.

Maxwell's death was an unplanned complication. As the weak link in the smuggling ring, the paranoid hotel clerk had become suspicious and tried to put me out of the way as a precaution. Riggson had killed him to protect me or to make himself appear totally law abiding; one who didn't want complete strangers being murdered in his hotel. That was another facet to which no one would ever know the true answer. Not even Jeff Street had been able to explain Maxwell's reasons for the actions leading to his death.

Sitting there in the heat, I was reviewing all the things

that had happened, when I heard the clicking of heels behind me.

"So you're leaving, too," Carol remarked. She set her two suitcases in line with the others on the veranda. "Mind if I sit down and smoke a cigarette?"

"My pleasure." I didn't tell her I had been looking for her. Instead, I dug into my shirt pocket for the pack of Luckies. I shook one half out of the pack and extended it toward her. Neither of us said anything until I had lit the cigarette. She blew a puff of smoke at the sun, which was slowly falling behind the roof of the courthouse.

"Where're you headed?" I finally asked.

"Los Angeles, I guess. Somewhere I can get a job. You and Barney put a sudden stop to things here."

I glanced at her to see if she was joking. She wasn't. She sat on the step with her nylon-clad knees crossed, critically eyeing the dust that eddied in the street. She saw me looking and covered her knees with the hem of the silk dress.

"This all has to be hard on you. You didn't ever suspect what was going on?"

She shook her head. "I still don't believe it. Chet always seemed so considerate. He just couldn't be as bad as some of the folks around here are saying."

I didn't share her feelings, of course. Riggson's car had been parked in the alley. It was pretty obvious he planned on herding me out the back door for a ride into the desert. He could have stuffed my body into a ditch or a crack, then covered it with one of his bulldozers. Everyone would figure I had just drifted on.

"His being so considerate of you is what first made me wonder," I told her. "Remember what you told me about

Riggson doing some of the office work himself at night? You said he did it to help you, but he never touched the stuff on your desk.''

She nodded, glancing curiously at me and then frowning. ''I remember.''

''It stood to reason he was handling something you didn't know about. And if he was eager enough to go down at night to write letters, keep books or whatever, he was making certain no one else knew what was going on.''

She was doubtful. ''That's not very much to go on.''

''Lots of little things added up in the end. I'll tell you about them sometime. What's the big attraction in L.A.?''

''Some kind of office job, I hope. That's about the only thing I'm qualified to handle.''

''Ever been to San Francisco?'' I asked. She shook her head and went back to staring at the dusty street.

''I know people there who should be able to help,'' I suggested. I saw the bus as it swung around the corner two blocks away. ''Why don't you go back in and change that ticket?''

She stared at me. Her introspective gaze suggested she was thinking it over.

''Why San Francisco, Sam?''

''That's where I'm going, and we need to know each other better. A lot better!''

I stood up and helped her to her feet.

''Hurry now,'' I ordered. ''This driver'll want to get moving.''

I helped the bus driver put the bags in the compartment in the belly of the vehicle while the other passengers got on. When we were done, I walked over to the door.

''You seem in a hurry to get on the way,'' the driver

commented. Carol came out of the hotel and down the steps, ticket in hand.

''Here's your last passenger,'' I told him.

We settled into the seats directly behind the driver. He shut the door, then ducked his head to study the sky. Big black clouds were rising up out of the desert to the south.

''Looks like we're going to get some rain,'' he ventured, as he put the bus in gear and we moved down the street. Carol reached over to take my hand in hers.

''You're wrong,'' I told him. ''It never rains this time of year. Never!''